PRETTY GURLS LOVE DOPE BOYS

PRECIOUS TAYLOR

TEXT UCP TO 22828 TO SUBSCRIBE TO OUR
MAILING LIST
If you would like to join our team, submit the first 3-4
chapters of your completed manuscript to
Submissions@UrbanChapterspublications.com

PROLOGUE

Josie AKA Jo'

I HID THERE, in the guest bathroom, with my body barely fitting under the sink. I was so ready to get from under this cramped space, but I knew that would have to wait until the Alberto Cartel was clear from my home. I had just snuck in the house an hour prior to our front door being kicked it. My parents and baby sister, Elena, were still peacefully sleeping as I heard the heavy footsteps raiding our home. I held my hand tightly over my mouth, being sure not to make a single noise. At this point, it was either me or my family. The Alberto Cartel didn't make home visits unless it was something that the person couldn't come back from. My parents had never been the type to do anything that would put our family into harm's way.

However, I do remember them discussing a plan with my

aunt and uncle on how to escape to the States. I only caught bits and pieces of the conversation before, but I was hoping this had nothing to do with it. Grasping me from my thoughts, I heard a loud scream release from my mother's mouth. My father and mother's bedroom was literally five feet from where I was hiding. Our home wasn't some great, big home. It literally had three bedrooms and one bathroom. My mom and dad just called the guestroom a guestroom to sound fancy, but really, it wasn't even setup as a bedroom. It still had boxes hiding out from where we hadn't unpacked certain things. The loud scream escaped my mother's mouth again, causing me to jump a little, but I quickly corrected myself when I realized what was at stake.

"You steal from your own kind, you must die," I heard a husky voice say.

"Please! No, please don't! Take me! She has nothing to do with it," I heard my dad crying out for help.

"Boss's orders. Your whole family must die. It does not matter who had anything to do with it. You put your whole family at risk when you stole money from the cartel. We trusted you. Our mistake," the husky voice said again.

Tears rolled down my cheeks as I heard my mother and father taking their last breath.

Pow! Pow!

I wanted so badly to jump from under that cabinet and hold my mother and father in my arms, but I just couldn't. I wasn't ready to die. I knew this was something I would live with on my conscience forever, but I'd rather live and make a difference than die behind someone else's mistake. No later did I hear my little sister's footsteps, assuming she had just heard what I heard. My little sister, Elena, was ten years old. I didn't think they would shoot an innocent child. They wouldn't do tha—My sentence was cut short when I heard another gunshot and what sounded like my baby sister's frail body hit the ground.

"All is done. We need to contact Faro and let him know," the husky voice said.

"Should we check home for more people?" what sounded like a woman's voice said.

How could a woman help someone kill a whole family in cold blood? I sat as still as I possibly could to not make a peep. As bad as this may seem, I didn't want to end up like my family. My soul left my body when I heard footsteps enter into the guestroom. Shadows crept between the cracks of the bathroom cabinet. I held my breath trying not to breathe or make any sudden movements. A phone began to ring from the person's pocket that was standing in front of the cabinet.

"Let's go! That was Faro. He needs us back to him in ten," the woman's voice said.

I almost jumped for joy when I heard the roaring from their truck pulling off into the Brazilian streets. I sat underneath the sink for at least another thirty minutes. I had to be sure the coast was completely clear. I pulled my cell phone out and sent a quick message to my best friend in the States, Cambria.

I'm coming to the States. I can't take it here anymore. See you soon.

It took her no time in replying.

Best news I've gotten all day. Great, I'll meet you at the airport in my city.

Cambria was someone I met through an online chat. We eventually became close after sharing our stories with each other. Cambria was twenty-two and living on her own in Atlanta. Her dad was a big-time drug dealer and very absent in her life, but he made sure she kept money and was well taken care of. She just hated the fact that no one was physically there for her family wise since her mother died of a drug overdose. She had a lot going on in her life, but she stayed levelheaded about every situation, and that's what I liked about her. She was my peace in the storm. She always told me that she had an extra room for whenever I wanted to get away. I never had the opportunity to actually travel the States until I went on a trip abroad my senior year in high school. My dad only agreed because it was for education purposes. My father didn't trust me much, so I was really surprised when he let me travel abroad. Luckily, my passport hasn't expired yet. Now it was my time to go.

Crawling from underneath the cramped space, I seen my baby sister's limp, lifeless body lying in the middle of our hallway in a puddle of blood. I walked over to her, planting a kiss on her forehead. I couldn't fight the tears. I was facing reality now that my family was no longer here with me. I stepped a few feet away to see my mother and father with bullet holes between their eyes. I wept, but I tried to keep myself together, which was such a struggle at this very moment. I reached in my dad's top drawer where he had his wallet. He had a total of three hundred dollars in there. I knew he wasn't going to need it now because... well, he was dead, so I took the money and stuck it in my pocket. I was so upset because this could've all been prevented, but I knew my dad had good intentions with his actions. I just hated it had to come to this.

I quickly ran to my small room I shared with my sister and packed a small, drawstring bag full of the few clothes I had and headed to the airport. I drove my dad's Oldsmobile and couldn't help but look in my rearview mirror every minute, hoping someone wasn't following me. When I finally pulled into the airport's parking lot, my mind was at ease. I grabbed all of my things from the car and headed inside to board a flight to Atlanta.

1

Josie "Jo'"

I HAD BEEN in the States for a few weeks and was still trying to get used to everything. I felt so refreshed, although the last vision I seen of my family flashed through my head every chance it got. I tried my hardest to push them to the back of my head. When Cambria pulled up to pick me up from the airport, I was so excited, so ready to start a new life. She looked exactly like her photos. I was just so thankful that she was willing to take me in and let me stay with her. Without her, I didn't know where I would be, because I know staying back home in Brazil would be no good for me, nor was it an option.

Before I met her, I didn't have any real friends. I was always working in my dad's shop or at home with my baby sister and mom. I was always alone if I wasn't with them. Most Brazilian families were strict, and some families where more lax than others. Our family was so close knit. We did everything together. I loved it. I was very sheltered, family oriented but laid back and willing to try new things all in the same note. I could tell Cambria was completely the opposite when she pulled up with her music blasting loud and driving full speed. Bria was the wilder of the two of us. Don't get me wrong, I knew how to have fun too, just probably not what Bria would've considered fun. I loved writing and reading. That was fun to me as to Bria partying was her best hobby. I didn't mind though. I was actually looking forward to opening up a bit and meeting new people.

"Hey, bitchhhhhh! I'm so happy you're finally here. I mean, of course, not on the circumstances, but we're going not to get through this together. I couldn't imagine being in your shoes right now. So I'm going to try my best to make this the best transition for you as possible. Is there anything specific you would want to do tonight? I know it's some parties we can go to. You need to keep your mind off what happened," Cambria said, plopping down on the bed next to me.

"Parties? How about something that involves being in the house? Only because I wouldn't want to be the party pooper and not enjoy myself fully because I barely know anyone." I wasn't knocking her for asking me to go to a party, because I knew she was just trying to help me cope with my current situation. I applauded her on that. That's what you call a real friend, but on the other hand, I also felt like going to a party was just too soon for me.

At least I thought so anyway. I knew she didn't mean any harm by it. I mean, people grieve in different ways, but that just wasn't one I was used to. I had been moping around the house ever since I got here. I just couldn't believe I no longer had any more family. Cambria was really the only person I had at this point.

"I'm sorry, Jo'. I didn't mean any harm by it. I'm so sorry. I just read somewhere online that the sooner you cope with some tragic shit that happened to you, the sooner you'll get over it. You've been moping around the house like a sad puppy since you've gotten here. I just wanted you to have some fun," Cambria said.

"Bria, I understand where you're coming from. I didn't say no to not doing anything, just not a party not tonight, please. Maybe tomorrow so I'll have more time to prepare myself," I admitted. Honestly, I didn't have many clothes to go partying in, and I didn't want Bria trying to provide everything for me.

"That's fine. Just know tomorrow I won't be taking no for an answer if I find another party. But hey, chilling in the house is better than nothing. I'm not trying to force you. I just want to pull you out of that depression phase before you fall in too deep. I love you, girl. Just remember, things happen for a reason. I'm here for you if you ever want to talk, and you know that. We might handle things differently, but I'm okay with that. I'm going to invite my brother and my boo over. It'll be real chill and laid back. You don't have to worry."

"Whatever you say, Bria," I said, turning my head to look out the window. Atlanta was such a beautiful place, and it was no denying that.

Bria's house was really nice too. It was a spacious condo. I was surprised by the vicinity. I don't know why I expected her to live somewhere different in something much smaller, considering that it was only her staying in the home. I guess not. Her house stood at two stories high, and we had to ride an elevator up to get to her door. It felt so classy riding an elevator just to get inside of your house. It made me feel rich. I know that sounded corny, but this house looked like we had literally stepped out of one home magazine to another.

"Why do you have this big home if it's just you here?" I asked, changing the subject.

"Girl, because I need my space. Plus, sometimes, I like sleeping in the different bedrooms. They are all decorated differently, so I'll feel like I'm in a different space whenever I want to be," Bria replied.

"It looks nice though, but it just seems like you're being extra to me," I added jokingly.

"Girl, when your daddy is the plug, you do what you want. Being extra is just me honestly. Ask anybody that really knows me. Go ahead and take your shower. I'll go ahead and call my brother and my boo up, and let them what time would be a good time for them to come over. I think since you don't want to go out, this would be a great time for you to meet somebody besides myself. Fresh, new start, here we come!" Bria jumped up and down for joy.

She seemed more excited than I did. I just let her enjoy her happiness. I was happy that she was trying to make me as happy as possible, so tonight, I was going to try to make the best out of this little gathering as I could. I just didn't know if I was 100% sure on meeting new people just yet. I was more the shy type than anything.

"Wait... I didn't say I wanted to meet anyone. I'm really shy when it comes to stuff like that. You know I wasn't really raised around men like at all except my father, and I mean, that's because he's my dad. I've never even had a boyfriend before. You know that, Bria!" I added.

I felt butterflies creeping in my stomach at the thought of meeting someone new. It seemed like Bria's mind was already set, and I couldn't renege on it now. I would just make the most of tonight. *It'll be over before I know it,* was all I kept preaching to myself in my head. I mean, that was how I looked at. As much as she was doing for me without a handout, the least I could do was chill with the guy she had setup for me. I mean, what would that hurt?

"Loosen up, Jo'. I wouldn't put you in a situation I wouldn't put myself in. Plus, you've had a long day, and it's time for you to wind down and relax. Plus, my brother is a nice, respectful guy. He would never do anything out of the way. I'd beat his ass. Now, come with me to my room. I'm sure I have something you can throw on that nice shape you have, girl. You need to show it off. God didn't give it to you for no reason," Bria said.

"Fine. You're lucky I love you," I told Bria as I followed behind her to her room. Her room was even bigger than her living room. I looked around the beautiful, pink satin room and felt like I was stepping from one magazine to another one again. I was so amazed. She was right. Every room in her home was decorated differently, and stepping into each room felt like I was in a whole other home.

Her home was nothing like I was used to. Her large, ceiling-to-floor windows overlooked downtown Atlanta. It was beyond beautiful. I kept catching myself drifting off into a daze. We stepped foot into her walk-in closet, and I swore everything she held up against my skin was absolutely beautiful. I guess it was a good thing too that I wasn't picky at all.

"Here, wear this. Simple but cute. It'll show your curves off," Bria insisted, handing me this black, strapless dress that barely came past my knees.

I quickly ran to the bathroom to freshen up, and I pulled the black dress on. She was right... it did show every curve that I didn't even know I had. I wasn't used to wearing things like this, but the black dress was doing me just right. I stood an even five-seven and weighed one hundred fifty pounds. I was always complimented on my smooth, toffee skin tone. My skin was always my best feature in my opinion because it was completely blemish free. My high cheekbones complimented my chinky eyes and soft, pink lips. The more I looked in the mirror, the more I started feeling myself as I let my hair fall down past my shoulders while applying some gloss that Bria gave me to my lips, and I struck a quick pose before I stepped out of the bathroom so Bria could see the final results. I was actually feeling a lot more confident in my look when her eyes almost popped out her head as she eyed me from head to toe.

"Hot mama! Go, best friend! That's my best friend! Damn, Jo', you coming like that!" Bria danced around me in circles, making me feel like money as she threw numerous compliments my way.

"Stop. I don't look that good, do I?" I questioned but was also serious because yeah, I felt good, but I wasn't used to dressing the way she had me dressed. My mother would never allow me to wear something so revealing. My mom was so conservative over everything. She believed the body was only for the man you were to marry. Don't get me wrong, I had no doubt in that, but it sure as hell felt good showing a little bit of skin. With the way Bria was complimenting me, I could almost guess the next word that we're going to come out of her mouth. I looked good as hell, and there was no denying that.

"You look perfect, bestie," Cambria said, planting a kiss on my cheek. Bria didn't look bad either. She had on a nude one-piece, and her short hair was laid to the gods. She told me they were finger waves, and she sure as hell was wearing it well. She had a nice body too. We were about the same size. We both had nice, long legs, flat stomachs, and small, perky breasts. When I heard her doorbell ring, that pulled me from my thoughts of comparing us to each other.

"Yay! They're here! Boo, just act like yourself. If you feel uncomfortable at any time, let me know." Bria jumped up and down for joy. Seeing her so hyped only made me more nervous.

"I'll try," I said dryly. I really didn't plan on meeting anybody or anybody trying to get to know me. I know I agreed to it, but it was only for Cambria. I don't want her to think I was stuck up. Plus, this was just a one-night thing anyway.

I followed behind Bria as she headed to the door. I was practicing in my head what I would say and how I would say it. I really didn't want to make a fool of myself. When she opened the door, I immediately locked eyes with the fine specimen of a man that was also known as Bria's fine ass brother. I couldn't hide the reddening in my cheeks. So I just left my head fall so it wouldn't be too noticeable.

"Hey, lil' mama. What's your name? I'm Fabio," Fabio said, licking his lips.

"Um. Hi. My name is..." My sentence trailed off, because for some reason, my name just wouldn't pop up in my head. This nigga had me speechless.

"Her name is Josie, but she goes by Jo'," Bria said, finishing my sentence for me.

"I'm sorry. I'm just a little shy," I admitted.

"Nah, that's cool, lil' mama. I'm not mad at you. I can tell you aren't from here though with your accent," Fabio said.

"Oh, yeah. I'm from Brazil," I said.

"That's what's up! I have family there, but I'm here because I wanted something different for myself. Brazil is nice and all, but being in the States is even better in my opinion," Fabio said.

"Well, maybe you could show me around sometime," I said. I almost shocked myself because it was being a bit bold for my own liking.

"I have no problem with carrying a shorty like you around the city," he said, flashing his pearly whites at me.

"Bria baby, I brought a bottle. I hope we aren't going to babysit it tonight," the man said that was all hugged up grabbing my best friend's ass.

"No, baby, no babysitting. Jo' needs to loosen up a bit. She has a lot going on. Jo', this is Cash, my boo. Marcus, this is Jo', my best friend," Bria said, introducing us.

"Nice to meet you. Tonight is about having fun. Forget what you had going on before we stepped foot in this crib and just chill. Trust me, we won't try you in any way. We have nothing but the utmost respect for Bria and her crib," Cash said.

"Right. Plus, we don't disrespect ladies," Fabio said, licking his lips. He was so damn fine to me. His strong, muscular build, fresh fade, nice, white teeth, and the sweatpants he had on revealed every piece of his shaft hanging between his legs. I felt my panties get moist.

"Hand me a glass. Let's get this party started," I said, trying to take my mind off his dick. We all poured up two shots in each glass, and we took them all to the head. This was my first time ever drinking. My dad would never allow this, even though I was grown, but tonight wasn't about restrictions. It was about having fun.

Fabio and I sat on one end of the couch while Bria and Marcus sat on the other end. Fabio and I were sitting so close, but I didn't mind it. He was fine as hell, and his cologne consumed my nose like fresh roses.

"So where yo' man at?" Fabio whispered in my ear.

"I don't have one. I never did," I replied.

"Wait... so you mean to tell me a woman as beautiful as you never had a man?" Fabio asked with a confused look on his face.

"I was so busy with my studies and trying to make it out of Brazil that I didn't have time. But now that I'm here to the States maybe—" I was cut short.

"Maybe I could be your man. I mean, I'm sure I could make you my lady," Fabio said as he rubbed his hand up my thigh.

"Oh, no... you probably have women lined up ready to sleep with you. Why would I want to be with someone like that?" I questioned honestly.

"Don't go based off my looks females throw themselves at me, but it's not about that. It's about who I'm allowing to get in my space. You're beautiful as hell, and I wouldn't pass you up. That would be dumb of me. Just get to know me," Fabio said, looking me in my eyes with sincerity. I looked away from him and seen that Bria and Marcus must've made it back to the bedroom. I turned my attention back to Fabio.

"I'm flattered, but you don't know me, Fabio," I stated honestly. I mean, yeah, he was fine as hell, but I had never had a male friend, let alone a boyfriend. I knew I was attracted to men, but my dad was always strict when it came to things like that.

"You're right. I don't know you, but I know enough. Cambria hasn't stopped talking about you since she met you. When she told me that she wanted me to meet you, I was surprised because she never ever approves of anybody when it comes to me. It should be the other way around because I'm her big brother, right? But as long as nobody harms her, we good. Now that you're fucking with us, the same applies for you. I'm not trying to come off strong, but when I see someone I want, I go for it," Fabio said.

"I was actually thinking the complete opposite about you coming off too strong. I find it attractive that you are so strong when it comes to communicating. Most guys aren't good with that... I don't think," I admitted, locking eyes with him. I grabbed the glass sitting in front of me on Cambria's table and took another shot of Hennessy. Although this was my first time drinking, it was starting to taste like water to me. I no longer felt the sober me, and I was fine with that. I trusted Fabio. Any man that was related to Cambria or that she brought around me, I knew they wouldn't try anything. Well, nothing that I didn't want to happen anyway.

"Well, that makes things even easier. We don't know each other like that, but like I said—" His sentence trailed off, I placed my finger over his lips and kissed his big, full, pink lips. Our tongues danced around in each other's mouths, and I pulled back quickly.

"I'm so sorry, Fabio. I don't know what came over me. I don't want you to think I'm one of those easy girls. I think the liquor just has me acting crazy," I said, feeling my face turn red. Something about him was bringing out a side of me I never witnessed before. I didn't know whether to like it or to apologize for my actions, so I just decided to say sorry.

"You good, ma. I'm not tripping. If your breath doesn't stink, we good. I'm not even the kissing type of nigga. I'm not tripping. Now, if you were some hoe that thought you was just gon' kiss me, you had another thing coming. Probably would've knocked your ass off this couch." Fabio chuckled, but I could tell he was serious. I was still embarrassed though.

He reached over and placed his warm hand on my thigh, causing the tiny hairs on the back of my neck to stand up. "Do you care if I do this?" Fabio asked, sliding my panties to the side and inserting his fingers into my honeypot. I didn't push his hand away because he was making my body feel a way I had never felt before, and I didn't want it to stop. I had never been with a man sexually, and this may seem crazy, but the liquor was definitely turning me on to him the more he danced with his fingers inside of me.

"Mhmm, it's fine," I moaned in a soft whisper. I didn't want Cambria to hear me. He sped up, causing my legs to shake uncontrollably while still being gentle at the same time. He then pulled his fingers out of my honeypot and stuck them in his mouth to taste me. My eyes locked with his as I waited for him to say something.

"Mmm. Sweet just like I expected," Fabio said. I did something I would have never done before. If I was back home, my parents wouldn't have even allowed me to be alone with a guy my age. My parents were so strict, but they didn't need to be because I knew what the expected of me. Now that I was on my own, I felt like it was time that I started living by my own rules and doing my own thing. Yes, I loved my family deeply, but I was grown, and this was now my life. So I was going to do what I wanted to... no matter what. Out with the old Josie, and in with the new Josie.

I stood up in front of him, grabbing his hand. I led him to the room I was going to be staying in. The way he was making me feel a few moments ago, I wasn't ready for it to end so soon. I wanted his fine ass to explore every inch of me while I did the same to him. I'm sure this was the liquor that had me moving the way I was, but I wasn't going to fight it, because a part of me also wanted it as bad as the liquor was making me want it, if that makes sense. I had been through so much in the last few days, between the incident in my hometown and traveling here. I just wanted to be free and not have to worry about anything or being judged on my actions. Maybe having sex would get my mind off everything. Shit, what did I know? I sure as hell was about to find out.

As soon as we entered the bedroom, Fabio took the initiative and laid me down on the bed while caressing and planting soft kisses on every inch of me. I was happy he took the lead because I really didn't know where to go from there. Pulling my dress and my panties off, I began to tense up a bit as he placed my legs on his shoulders while he used his tongue to satisfy me. Arching my back, I felt myself about to climax. Wrapping his arms around my back, he gave me no room to escape. The way this man was pleasing me, I had never felt so good.

"Relax, ma, let me enjoy you. But tell me if you want me to stop because I will. Don't want you to feel like I'm forcing myself on you or whatever," Fabio grunted against my cat. The warmth from his mouth took me to another level. I felt like I was in another dimension. I could tell he was drunk by the way his words slurred as he spoke to me, but it didn't matter because I was too.

"No, don't stop," I replied almost above a whisper.

"You sure? I don't want you doing something you don't

want to," Fabio assured me as he sat up a little bit more so he could make direct eye contact with me.

"I'm positive. Be gentle with me is my only request," I moaned as he went back down on me, tearing my center piece to shreds with his tongue. I loved how he made sure I was completely OK with him and what we were doing before he continued. It showed me that he really did have respect for women, although I did have a thought in the back of my head wondering if he did this often.

"I'll go slow. Your wish is my command," Fabio said as he pulled his boxers down and revealed the sledgehammer he had between his legs. I cocked my head to the side for a second to make sure I was really seeing what I thought I was. I was so amazed at how large his manhood was, but in the same breath, I was scared because I was still a virgin. I didn't feel the need to share that with him right then because we had already gotten this far. I didn't want to mess the mood up.

"Umm," I choked up and finally said.

"Don't worry. I know I'm packing, but I'll be gentle with you just like you asked. At any time, let me know if you want me to stop, because I will." Fabio reminded me.

"No, come on." Pulling him by his T-shirt, he landed right on top of me. I opened my legs as far as they would go, welcoming him in.

Slowly entering himself inside of me, my body's automatic reaction was to tense up. I wasn't used to this, but I tried to relax as much as possible. It hurt the first few strokes, but after the fourth stroke, it felt amazing. Fabio was dipping in and out of me with his whole nine inches of dick.

"Fuck, lil' mama. You tight as hell, 'bout to make a nigga fall in love, and I didn't even bust yet."

"Oh my God, Fab! I'm about to cum! Fuck me! Harder," I moaned as he turned me over on my stomach and entered me from behind. The dick he had was like magic. I turned back to look at him, and with each stroke, his dick was covered with my juices.

"You like this dick, baby?" Fabio grunted as I felt his dick jump inside of me.

"Yesss! I do, papi! Fuck me!" I bit down into the pillow. I didn't know what was coming over me, but I loved the side Fabio was bringing out of me.

I placed my face back in the pillow and let him take control as he pounded me from the back, speeding up with each stroke. As Fabio made love to me, he maneuvered his hands all over my body. It felt so right. My toes began to curl with each stroke as he switched me to different positions. This nigga had me wrapped like a pretzel. Feeling my body climax for what seemed to be the fifth time, I tightened my legs around his waist as he pounded my kitty vigorously.

"I'm about to bust," Fabio said, grunting harder, and I soon felt his body limp over top of mine. He rolled over and grabbed my chin and pulled me closer to him placing a kiss on my forehead then my lips. He cuddled me close to him. Everything felt so right, and I didn't want this to end at all. I felt the sleep finally approaching, and I passed out in his arms.

Waking up butt naked and not seeing Fabio lying beside me, I was a little confused because he didn't say goodbye. He just left his number on my nightstand. On the other hand, I was glad he left. I didn't want Bria to think that I was easy. Although she did set us up, I didn't know how she would feel about us sleeping together. I didn't even know how to feel about it.

I lay there in my bed underneath the covers, thinking about the prior night's actions. I wasn't ashamed at all, because it seemed like we both wanted it. In reality, I didn't know how to feel about the situation, but I wasn't going to dwell on it. I would just look at it as my first wild night in Atlanta. Quickly hopping in the shower, I felt so relieved letting the steaming-hot water run down my back. Before I could get too deep into my thoughts, I heard a few loud knocks at the bathroom door, almost causing me to jump out of my skin.

"Best, hurry up! I want to take you shopping for something new. Plus, you need a phone. I can't have you out here without a phone. You're too cute, bitch. Somebody might snatch your pretty ass up. I can't have my best friend walking around here looking crazy, period!" Bria said, screaming from behind the closed door.

I really didn't want Bria doing anything for me money wise. I really wanted to get on my feet on my own, but I knew if I went against going shopping with her, she would do nothing but shut that down.

"I'll be down in a second," I replied. I finished bathing and reached for my bag that was lying on the dresser drawer nearby. I huffed as I searched through the three outfits that I had brought with me as if more was going to reappear out of thin air. I huffed. I knew they weren't nearly good enough to go on a shopping date with Bria. I sat on the edge of the bed for a few minutes and pondered in thought. I grabbed a pair of pants I had and cut them into shorts with some scissors I found in the bathroom. I tied my T-shirt in a knot in the front and spun around in the mirror. I was a little bit more satisfied than what I thought I would be. I pulled my hair up into a bun, laying my bangs neatly on my face.

"Finally. It took you forever. But bitch, you look great," Bria said, turning around to examine my outfit before grabbing my hand and placing a kiss on my cheek.

"Thank you. You really think so? It literally took me ten minutes to make." I revealed as I took a bite into an apple that was sitting on Bria's countertop.

"Girl, yes! Now you should know by now I wouldn't lie to you. I was almost worried about yo' ass up there," Bria admitted.

"Shut up. Where are we going?" I asked.

"The mall, honey. They have a lot of stores in just one spot. That's why I love being there. Enough of the sweet talk... tell me about you and my brother. What do you think of Fab?" Bria asked as we headed out to her car.

I could almost feel my face turning red at the sound of his name. I sat for a moment, replaying the events that happened the prior night in my head before I decided to answer.

"He's cute or whatever. I like his vibe," I admitted, keeping it short and sweet. Honestly, it wasn't even much for me to tell. Well, it was a lot that I could've told her, but I wanted to talk to him again before I made any judgments on him or shared what happened between me and him with her. Bria was my best friend true, but I just didn't know if it was worth telling her, because maybe it wasn't a big deal to Fab as much as it was me.

"Girl, byeee! You were all over him last night. I'm surprised that's all you have to say about him." Bria chuckled.

"OK, and I don't see how you were even watching what I was doing when your face was buried all up your boo's ass." I shot back at her lurking ass. I was picking up on Bria's attitude, and I think it was starting to rub off on me. I was saying things and doing things that I wouldn't normally do. But I wasn't complaining. I was enjoying the woman I was becoming.

"Girl, Cash is cool and all, but I don't know. Sometimes

he just pisses me off so bad." Bria didn't even take her attention off the road as we pulled into the mall's parking lot. I could see it was something that happened last night that made her feel some type of way, and it wasn't good.

"Hm, sounds good. He sure wasn't pissing you off last night." I tried to lighten the mood a little bit because I could see the conversation was going somewhere she didn't really want it to go.

"He's just some dick when I need it. I mean, don't get me wrong, I do really love him, but last night, his phone kept ringing, and it was his ex-girlfriend. He been told me that he cut her off and that it was no more communication between the two, but I see he was just lying. I didn't mention it to him, because his ass wasn't going to do anything but lie again. It's like that's all he knew how to do like I'm some dumb ass bitch. Long story short, niggas aren't shit. Next subject," Bria said, leading the way into this clothing store that looked like it sold nothing but clothes that were made specifically to cling to your ass and breasts.

As badly as I wanted to ask her about what really happened between her and Cash, I knew she was giving off signals that she wanted me to just leave it where it was at. So I did. Bria always talked about Cash and how she loved him so much before I came to the States, but of course I was never able to put a face with a name until last night when him and Fab came over. Cash didn't seem like he would be Bria's type liked she deserved.

He seemed too rough around the edges, and he had tattoos all over his body. Well, the parts that I could see had tattoos running up and down his neck and arms. I sure if he was bold enough to have them on his neck and face, he would have them everywhere else. He had this natural mean mug on his face that Bria told me about, but I thought she was just kidding until I saw him last night. He had a gun on his hip and an olive-green Nike sweat suit that fit perfectly. He had gold teeth in and gold chains on. His attitude was even rough, but he just didn't seem like Bria's type in my eyes. But then again, she did have a wild side to her and maybe that complemented her in her eyes, but if he was hurting her, then she needed to let his ass go. It was more fish in the sea.

"This would look really cute on you, girl." Bria held up this black, leather mini skirt against my waist. It was cute, but I never wore something so revealing before.

"Yes, this is cute, but I don't have any money right now, and I don't want you paying for it," I stated bashfully, trying to downplay the fact that I didn't know if I would be comfortable in it either.

"Girl, bye. Didn't I tell you before my daddy is the plug? If I got you, I got you. Plus, my brother Fab is having a party tonight at Club Ramos, and he wants us to come, so you need to look the best of the best. Now, go try it on," Bria added.

"Wait. Huh? Party? Fab?" I blurted out.

"Calm down. It'll be fine. I know you haven't been to a

club before, so I decided to surprise you. Plus, I figured you would like to see Fab's ugly ass again. Since you couldn't keep your hands off him," Bria said.

Oh my God! What did she mean by that? My mind immediately started to wander. *What if he told her what happened between us before I got the chance to?* The last thing I wanted was her to think I was keeping things from her. Well, then again, I could've just been overreacting. If she knew anything, I'm sure she would ask me. That's just the type of person she was. I got out of my head and started enjoying this little shopping spree because I sure did need it, and if I was going to see Fabio tonight, I wanted to look the best of the best just because. What could I say? I did have a little crush on him. Is that so bad?

2

Cambria "Bria"

Jo' and I had about an hour and some change to finish getting ready. She was acting all weird when I mentioned Fab's name, but I just assumed that was because she really liked him. I knew she would though. My brother was hard to not like. I was psyched about going to the party, but it definitely wasn't to see Cash's ass. I just wanted him to see how good I was going to look. I was so tired of that nigga playing with my image it made me so sick. I loved him with everything in me, and I would do just about anything for him, and it just seemed like that wasn't good enough. Cash knew that, so I really couldn't understand why he was so caught up in trying to impress these lame ass bitches that couldn't do shit for him. I was starting to feel like I was reaching my breaking point with him, but a part of me still wanted him to change and do right. He acted as if the ground he walked on was supposed to be kissed. He wanted me to be accepting to all of his bullshit, and that just wasn't me. At all. I wasn't that type of bitch, and I wasn't about to start being that type. I loved Cash with everything in me, but he just didn't know how to act, and I was getting fed up.

Tonight was all about popping out on his ass and showing him that I could have any nigga I wanted in hopes of him seeing that and getting his act together. I know that may seem crazy, but shit, I was crazy, so what? Everybody knew Cash was my nigga, and that's how it was always going to be until I said otherwise.

I stepped into my red, fitted, strapless dress and stepped into my black red bottoms. I was definitely feeling like money. I smiled in satisfaction because I knew Cash wouldn't be able to keep his hands off of me. I loved giving that nigga a run for his money, especially when he acted like he forgot who the fuck I was. Cash and my brother, Fab, were really close. We practically all grew up together, but the strange thing about it was Fab always lived with his dad

up until we turned seven years old.

I would always remember him coming down here to visit for our summer months out of school and then leave again to go back home. I know you're probably wondering how Fab and I are so close if he didn't stay down here long, and how did my dad take it with my mom having a child near the same age as me somewhere else? My mom was paid a lot of money to be a surrogate when I was younger. My mom kept in touch with Fabio's mom up until she passed away when Fabio was seven years old, and that's when he came to stay with us.

My dad was pretty cool with it because he always wanted a little boy, and my mom told him that she was set in stone on not having any more kids. Fabio's dad became depressed and didn't have time to take care of Fabio, so that's why he came to stay with us. Well, that's what my mom told us as we got older. I never questioned it because my mom would never lie to me.

Fabio was just like a real brother to me though. He protected me, nurtured me, and made sure no nigga ever made a fool of me. My brother's face card was really good in the streets, and everyone respected him. If he knew what Cash's dumb ass was doing, he would have his head on a silver platter. Yeah, they were best friends, but Fabio was always blood before anybody. That was just his loyalty, and that's what made us so much closer.

There was a soft knock at my door, and I knew it was Josie. She was still trying to warm up to being here, so she was acting all shy and shit. I'd give her ass a few more days with my brother, and she wouldn't be on that shy shit anymore.

"What do you think of this, Bria, and be serious?" Jo' said, doing a spin showing off her outfit. She had on the leather mini skirt I picked out for her with a white halter top that revealed her cleavage.

"You really do look good when you dress up, best friend." I was complimenting her. She had that natural glow. She didn't even need makeup, but I wanted to try some on her to see how much more beautiful she could get. "You should let me try some makeup on you," I said.

"Bria, you always boosting me. Now you want to doll me all up," Jo said, rolling her eyes.

"So I didn't hear a no," I said, gently pulling her over to my vanity. I loved makeup. It was my life. I loved looking good. I dolled Jo' up real good, nothing too dramatic because she already had the cute, baby face.

When we pulled up to the club, I could hear the sound of the music coming through the parking lot of the club. The line was long outside, but good thing Fabio had a pair of VIP tickets for us. I never waited in the long lines, and I always had Fabio to thank for that. He had so many connects throughout Atlanta it didn't make no sense. My dad raised Fabio up into the game. He was pretty much like my dad's right-hand man besides my uncle Gutta.

Gutta was like a second dad to us. He held shit down when my dad had to go away for a little bit to do time. I was so thankful for him because he kept everything running smooth like Daddy was never gone. My dad did some time for beating some dude so bad he was in a coma and was paralyzed from the neck down. He didn't even want to press charges when he came up out of his coma, so they had to drop the charges, and my daddy was a free man back out doing what he used to.

"Bitch, come on. What are you day dreaming about?" Jo' said, pulling me from my thoughts.

"I'm sorry, girl. Come on," I said as we walked through the crowd, heading up to the VIP section.

All eyes were on us, and I didn't mind soaking that up. I loved being seen. I knew if these niggas seen me, Cash was somewhere in a corner eyeing me. We finally made it to the section, pushing through the traffic. My brother was sitting in the booth vibing and drinking the Patrón right out the bottle.

"Nigga, you better slow down on all of that. I know it's your birthday, but ain't nobody in here carrying yo' big ass out of here, and you need to stay on your game," I said, hitting Fabio upside the back of his head. My brother was hated by many, and he didn't need to be out here just falling off his pivot.

"Shut up, Bria before I get on yo' ass about that little ass dress. Move now, and enjoy yourself," Fabio said, brushing past me to hug on Jo'. I just ignored his comment because I knew what was best for him, and he knew that. I was a little upset he pulled Jo' away, and now my ass was an easy target for Cash's dumb ass.

I sat in the booth pouring up a shot as I swayed my hips back and forth against the chair. The liquor was so smooth, and I was just starting to feel myself when Cash walked up. I was sure about to give his ass a hard time.

After going through his shit, I was over him. I was so tired of the same tired ass games this nigga was playing. He wasn't going to have his cake and eat it too fucking with me. I wasn't that type of bitch. Yeah, I loved him, but I loved myself more.

"What I tell you about coming out the house looking too good?" Cash whispered in my ear, and he slid into the booth next to me.

"Nigga, I don't listen to you or anybody else. I go with my own flow," I said, still looking out into the crowd and taking another sip of my drink. My brother and I loved Patrón. That was our turn-up juice for any special occasion.

"Look, baby girl, I understand you're upset, but..." Cash's voice trailed off as I stood up and walked away from him. I really was tired of hearing that same old speech. He said the same thing every time, apologizing about being dumb and knowing that what he did was dumb. But see, the part he could never explain was why he kept doing it. Until he could truly change his ways for me, he didn't deserve my time.

As I walked to the banister, someone approached me. I couldn't really tell from afar, but he looked good as hell. He was tall and had a Hershey's chocolate complexion. He smiled at me, turning his hat from the front to the back, and revealing his full face. He shot me a smile full of gold teeth that was to die for. The accent he carried put the cherry on the top as I felt my panties moisten. I shot Cash a look to see if he was watching me, which he was. Cash wasn't the type of nigga to interrupt. He was going to sit back and watch how it all played out before he made a move. I grabbed the guy's hand and pulled him somewhere we wouldn't be watched like a hawk. As much as I wanted to torture Cash, another part of me really wanted to see what this other brother was talking about.

"Hey, my name is A'Koni, but everybody calls me AK," the fine specimen of a man said to me, introducing himself.

"My na-na-name is..." I paused for a second because why the hell was I stuttering? Yeah, he was fine as hell but not enough to have me tripped up on my words. Or was he?

"Chill, mama. I won't bite... unless you want me to," he said, throwing a smile at me again that was absolutely to die for.

"My name is Cambria, but everybody calls me Bria," I said.

Before he could say anything, Cash came up with the butt of his gun, hitting A'Koni's temple. He smacked him with the butt of the gun multiple times until he saw blood.

"Cash! Stop! What the fuck is wrong with you!" I screamed at the top of my lungs. I knew no one could hear me over the loud music, but motherfuckers was just standing by watching like they couldn't break it up. I'd never seen this side of Cash, and honestly, I wasn't really liking it.

"Yo, chill! What the fuck you doing, Cash? Get yo' ass up, man!" Fabio said, pushing between me and pulling Cash up off of A'Koni's almost-unconscious body.

"Bro, he was all on Bria, bruh. She was entertaining that shit too much. You know how I am about her," Cash said, cutting his eyes at me.

"Nigga, that don't mean you get out here on that nut shit. You were beating that man with the pistol for almost ten minutes straight. This my lil' sis, but y'all need to tighten the fuck up. All this extra, childish shit is lame!" Fabio said, helping A'Koni up off the ground.

I just walked away and went to find Jo'. I knew she would be somewhere nearby. I wasn't trying to be a party pooper, but I was ready to go. Cash just ruined my whole night. Now wouldn't nobody give me any attention because they wouldn't want to be beating Cash's stupid ass.

"Bitch, come with me to the bathroom," I said into Jo's ear. I hate that I interrupted her and Fab's bonding with my bullshit, but it was what it was. I needed her more. Fab needed to get his little friend Cash together before I stabbed his stupid ass.

"I thought you would never ask. I've been holding my pee since I got with your brother. Something about him made me nervous, and when I get nervous, I have to pee," Jo' said, following behind me to the bathroom.

"At least you're enjoying your night somewhat. I'm getting real irritated with Cash. Like no, I didn't want to talk about it before, but now I do before I go upside his stupid ass head."

"I'm sorry he's ruining your night, best friend. You don't deserve that. You know if you want to talk, I'm here for you," Jo' said.

"It's just like I really love Cash with everything in me. It just hurts me so bad that he can sit in my face and lie to me just as if nothing has happened. Every time I feel like we're getting somewhere, it feels like we're being pushed back ten more feet. When I went through his phone, I found out he had been fucking with multiple other bitches. He had one feeling so comfortable she was asking him about me." I let my head fall. I was feeling so ashamed. But I knew we were in the club, and I needed to tighten up. As soon as Jo' was about to respond, a short, light-skinned girl stepped from the stall.

I didn't even notice anybody was in here, Jo' mouthed to me.

"Sweetie, the first thing you can do is stop all that crying, and realize that Cash will never love yo' young ass," the strange, light-skinned woman said.

"Excuse me, bitch?" I questioned because she met her fucking match today, coming at me sideways and jumping in my shit like she knew me.

"Bitch, you heard what I said. Cash is my nigga. He may have your nose wide open, but believe me, his nose wide the fuck open about me. By the way, my name is Hennessy. Remember that, baby, because this won't be the last you hear from me," Hennessy said, heading toward the exit.

"Aht, aht, bitch. Not so soon. What the fuck was that shit you was talking?" I said in the calmest voice possible while dragging her by her raggedy ass wig across the bathroom floor.

"Get the fuck off of me! You dirty ass bitch!" Hennessy cried.

"Dirty is the last thing you should speak upon me, bitch!" I continued punching the bird bitch in her mouth until I seen blood. I blacked completely the fuck out. Before I knew it, Jo' was pulling me off of her because the girl was now laying their unconscious.

"Bria, look what you did! Oh my God! She's not responding! What do we do?" Jo' cried.

Whew! My friend was really acting like a little bitch. I was definitely about to bring her up out of that stage. I was a pretty girl, but I wasn't raised to let anybody disrespect me, and that was just that. Bitches used to step out of line to me all the time, until I beat this one bitch so bad she was in the hospital for days. I was facing small charges behind that, but it wasn't nothing I couldn't beat. I was actually surprised that bird stepped to me the way she did. She was bold, especially behind Cash's ass. Everybody knew that man was in love with me, and if I was the one to be completely done, his ass wouldn't know how to act. But that bitch was the main reason I couldn't even do it with Cash anymore. He had too many females out here feeling comfortable and extra froggy. Something I was definitely good on.

"Hello? Bria!" Jo' screamed, dragging me from my thoughts.

"Bitch, shut up! Fuck her! Let's go have fun." I did want to leave before, but that bitch Hennessy gave me a reason to turn this club the fuck up.

I walked over to the sink to wash my hands. I felt Jo' staring at me, but this was just something she was going to have to get used to if bitches continued to try my character. Sooner or later, she would be on the same shit I'm on, especially if she was fucking with my brother. Grabbing Jo's hand, I pushed through the crowd where my brother was standing. We danced, drank, and danced some more until it was time for us to head home.

When we finally got back to the house, I couldn't be happier to be in my bed with my feet kicked up, smoking a blunt. For some reason, I felt like a weight had been lifted off my shoulders.

3

Hennessy

Leaving the club with Cash was what I intended on doing anyway. He had been fucking with that little girl, Cambria, for too long. It was time for me to snatch my man up like I should've been did when I met him in the club two years ago. We'd been through this back and forth shit, so it was nothing new to me. I noticed Cambria's ass there when I was making my way up to his section. She was right up his ass like he expected.

Cash was so drunk at the club after Cambria left that I found that as my opportunity to lure him back home. You know, just making sure he got there safely. Cash and I weren't dating anymore, but I sure as hell wasn't about to let another bitch have him. This Cambria girl had been in the picture for years before I even came around, but that didn't even matter to me. Her time was up, and it was time for me and Cash to live happily.

I met Cash at the club, our mutual meeting grounds. We were always there having fun and turning up. I loved partying, and I guess that's why Cash fucked with me because I knew how to have fun, unlike Cambria's boring ass. I knew he had a girl when I first talked to him. I mean, who didn't know Cash? He was the most well-known nigga in the streets. Him and Fab ran Atlanta. The reason I didn't give a fuck about him having a girlfriend was because my logic was if he cared anything about her, he wouldn't have approached me and fucked me raw the same night he met me. That's just how I looked at it.

"Cash, daddy, wake up. You want me to give you some head?" I cooed in his ear as if he was going to reply. This nigga was knocked out cold. He always partied hard and would sleep all day the next day if you let him. This head game was crazy, or so I'd been told, so I knew he would be excited to wake up to it.

As he lay there in a pair of his Ralph Lauren Polo boxers, I jumped on top of him, pulling the covers back and eyeing his dick like I was at the meat market. Cash was packing in more than one way. I think that's why I was so hooked on him. That man could really lay some pipe. Truthfully, he was some of the best dick I'd ever had, and I was thirty. So that had a lot to say about men my age.

I turned my attention back to Cash's manhood as I licked my lips in admiration. This man looked good enough to eat, so that's exactly what I was going to do. Eat that dick! Suck my man from soft to hard with no complications. Cash loved when I did that.

"Fuck, Henn." Cash grabbed the back of my head as I stroked his dick with my mouth like a blowfish. The sound of him moaning was turning me on even more as I covered his dick with my saliva.

I sucked his dick and fucked him whenever he wanted. I came running whenever he needed me. I even got evicted from my apartment because of him. I was so tied up running behind him I lost my job, and one thing just crumbled after another. I was so thankful for my cousin Nicki because without her, I would be on the streets somewhere.

Cash filled a void for me that I didn't want to lose ever. The way he made me feel when we were together was unexplainable. I just longed to be loved by him, be with him, and have his cute, little babies. A few months after me and Cash started messing around, I ended up getting pregnant, but I let him talk me into getting an abortion, and after that I noticed it had become a continuous pattern. Abortion after abortion, and it was starting to take a toll on my body, so I decided to get on birth control until he was ready. I knew Cash loved me and wanted me, but he just had a weird way of showing it.

I was still madly in love with Cash, and he knew that because I told him numerous times. However, for some odd reason, he would never take it there with me. No matter how many times I begged and pleaded, he just wouldn't make it official. I tried to stop giving a fuck a few months ago, but it was hard when we were still fucking from time to time. I jumped out my feelings and snatched his soul just as I would normally do, shaking the bitter thoughts from my head and applying that pressure on him with my head-game skills.

I let Cash bust all over my face, and I got up and headed to the bathroom to wash it all off. "Daddy, you hungry?" I called out to Cash, but he didn't answer. When I went back in the bedroom, he was gone, I picked up my phone about to text him until I seen he had already told me to let myself out and not be there when he got back.

I sat on the bed and huffed for a moment. I wondered what his ass was up to today. I wasn't about to sit around and find ways to stalk him, not today. I didn't have time. Although I would enjoy that, I was going to meet with my cousin, Nicki, and my best friend, Bonnie. The three of us was nothing but hell on wheels when we got up, and I think that's why we all got along so well because we knew how to turn shit up and shut shit down within the blink of an eye.

I was mad Bonnie couldn't come out with me last night because her ass was booed up with Gutta's ass. Yes, Fab's uncle. Gutta had Bonnie's ass on lock. Not too many people knew they were fucking around, but that's how they liked it, and I didn't know why. We all had our select picks out the bunch. When I said I met Cash at the club, I meant the strip club. Bonnie and I used to dance together. That's how we knew each other. Nicki used to dance with us too until she got popped by Fab, but that's another story for another time.

If Bonnie's ass was with me last night, then we would've tag teamed and beat the dog shit out of Cambria's sad, puppy ass. I left Cash's house and headed straight to mine because the longer I sat, the more I was going to want to track his ass down and curse him out for leaving me without a proper goodbye. Instead, I decided to call Bonnie on the way home because I knew she would talk me out of it.

"Hey, best friend!" I yelled into the phone as soon as the line connected. Ever since Bonnie got a new job dancing and quit the strip club we met at, I hadn't really been in touch with her much. I missed my bitch so much.

"Hey, best! I miss you so much. I'm off this weekend, so we need to do something. No matter what it is, I'm ready to turn the fuck up! Dancing just isn't the same without you, Henn. You need to come to Dallas with me and dance," Bonnie exclaimed.

"Chile, bye. You know I can't leave Cash. As bad as I would love to be down there making some real money, I just can't right now, but as far as turning up tonight? Now you're talking my language. Girl, I just left Cash's crib. I'm heading to mine now. This motherfucker gon' leave right after I suck his dick. Didn't even have the audacity to tell me bye or nothing. Can you believe that shit?" I went on a small rant.

"Bitch, first of all, you know I can believe that, but what I can't believe is why you're still fucking with his lame ass. I told you to come to the older side and get you a grown ass man. Ain't no way no twenty-something-year-old would have me down bad like his ass has you. I don't know why you still fucking with his ain't-shit ass anyway. He literally treats you like shit. You must like shit because that's how you are coming behind him. You're too cute for him. How many times do I have to tell you this? But shit, whatever rocks your boat." Bonnie spat, but I could tell she was upset because the hostility in her voice was at an all-time high.

The crazy part is I could've been living my best life in Dallas with Bonnie, and she was right; I did deserve better, but the heart wants what the heart wants. Bonnie never liked Cash after she realized he made me have an abortion for the third time. She would always preach to me about how I deserved better and how having so many abortions wasn't doing anything but damaging my body. Trust me, I knew now.

I really tried not to think about it so much, because I loved Cash, and I didn't need anybody throwing their two cents in my business—best friend or not. I was going to do what I wanted to do when it came to Cash. and clearly, I thought everyone should've known that by now. I was starting to regret even bringing it up to her.

"He's twenty-five, but age has nothing to do with anything. Anyway, you ready to get your head snatched, honey? It's long overdue for me." I changed the subject and looked in my mirror. I looked a hot mess. I felt like one too when my hair wasn't done. I was tired of walking around here looking like who did it and why. I just knew my girl Kita was about to have my hair laid and slayed as always.

"Don't try to change the subject, Henn. You need to tighten up before it's too late. I don't know what happened to the old Henn I knew, but I want my bitch back. I'll leave it at that though. But I'm more than ready. I been wearing this damn ponytail for a week too long. I just didn't feel like going to anybody in Dallas, because you know how I am about my hair. I don't want motherfuckers playing in my shit."

"Whatever. I'll change whatever I want. Damn, girl, three weeks though? Nah, I feel you because I would've been holding out too. I don't have time. Ever since Kit burned my hair out with that damn dryer, I said never again. Anyway, tell me how your new job is.? Do you like it?"

"I love it actually. Quick, fast, easy money, and I really can't complain. Just wish my girl was there with me. Besides that, you know I love dancing and all attention being on me anyway, so you knew this job was right up my alley when Gutta put me on," Bonnie said.

"I knew you would, and I know. Shit, I wouldn't mind making some quick money. I might come up there for a weekend. I said might, so don't get your hopes up. I still feel like Gutta took you to Dallas to keep you away from yo' bitches. I would get a job down here, but I'm alright with scamming niggas. It is doing me just fine," I replied bluntly.

"Gutta is trying to put me in a position to win. That's what you need out of a nigga—somebody that's going to help you win, not somebody that's going to use yo' ass until they can't use you no more. I'm trying to give you free game, honey. That shit you got going on with that man is going to come back and bite you in the ass one day. You need to just let that shit go and come dance with me. Your body is snatched to the gods. You'll make a lot of money. I'm trying to tell you," Bonnie insisted.

"Girl, I'm pulling up at the house. I'll meet you at the hair salon, and don't mention a job to me again. I said I'm good doing what I'm doing, best, and if you don't have something nice to say about Cash, let's just not even speak on it," I said and disconnected the call before she could say anything more. Bonnie was my best friend, and I loved her, but I think the real reason I wasn't trying to hear what she had to say was because she had some truth in what she was saying, and I wasn't ready to face that.

I ran up the stairs to my cousin Nicki's house. She let me move in with her a few months back when I got evicted from my apartment. Don't get me wrong, scamming niggas was great money, but it wasn't always a scamming nigga available at the last minute anyway. When I lost my apartment, that shit broke me to pieces because that was the only thing besides my car that I had in my name.

The only reason I even had the car was because my mom gave it to me before she started hitting the bag heavy. I was glad she signed it over to me than her boyfriend, Tommy. He's the one that got her on that shit. She started a few years ago, and everyone was saying they saw her down at the bottom store trying to get a bag, but I didn't want to believe it until I saw it with my own eyes. One day, I popped up at her house without her knowing and saw her shoving the white dust up her nose.

I was mad at myself that I didn't get her any help sooner, but Cash was there to comfort me through that time. He explained to me that it wasn't anything I could do about it because she was already too far gone. I just prayed she got the help she needed. Ever since I caught her with her face buried deep in that shit, I hadn't talked to her since, so I didn't know if she was dead or alive.

I thought it would be best if I cut my mom completely off because I didn't need that type of negativity in my life. Every day, I would sit and try to put two and two together on when things exactly went wrong with my mom, but I couldn't seem to put my finger on it. She was never the type to do any kind of drugs or spend her time with a dude like Tommy. My mom was a sweet, easy-going woman who stayed to herself, so how she even came across Tommy was still unknown to me.

One day, I just woke up, and she was a different person.

Bad thing about it was I never got to sit down and ask her why. I just knew she gave up on everything and anything once I seen her doing the drugs for myself. I was wondering why my mom had started losing so much weight, but I just assumed it was old age. When I realized that wasn't the reason, I gave up on her. My cousin was my left hand, we did everything together growing up, and she always made sure I was straight, and for that, I would always look out for her like she was a sister.

"Cousin, is that you?" Nicki called from the kitchen.

"Yes, bitch, it's me. You better not have anybody else just walking up in here freely where my niece lay her head."

"Hey, Auntie! I've missed you," Aubrey said, running up and wrapping her arms around my neck as I squatted down and gave her a hug.

"Girl, I'm grown as fuck. Chill out. Brey, baby, go play in your room for a little bit while I talk to auntie. Grandma will be coming to get you soon, so I'll be up there to get you packed and ready, alright, baby?" Nicki said to Aubrey.

I loved my niece to death. I would do anything in the world for that little girl. I guess that was because she was the only person that looked up to me and made me feel like this life shit was worth it.

Sometimes I looked at Aubrey and wondered what it would be like if Cash and I had a baby. I mean, I wasn't a bad person, and I'm sure I would've been the best mother. I still got in my feelings about my previous abortions. I had all of the ultrasounds from each abortion appointment in a pocket in my purse. Nicki didn't know about the abortions, just Bonnie, but that's how I wanted to keep it. Nicki was so judgmental, and now that I actually thought about it, I wished I wouldn't had told Bonnie, because every chance she got, she was coming at me crazy about him. I felt so bad about it sometimes when Bonnie would bring it up because I didn't want to kill those babies. That was never my initial plan. I wanted to have a family with Cash, but I knew if anything, he knew the correct timing to have a child, and he knew what was best for us, and I left it at that.

"What's up? What do we need to talk about?" I questioned Nicki because if it was about Cash, I didn't want to hear it.

"Girl, so I heard Fab's uncle Gutta ass is having a birthday bash tonight, and ladies are free. You know Cash and Fab will be there, and I'm sure them bitches will be too. We can run down on they ass. If we get the chance, cool. If not, we can shake the table a little bit." Nicki rubbed her hands together as if she had just come up with a master plan, but little did she know, she had just hit the motherfucking jackpot.

"Wait a minute, bitch, because I really think you just did something. I was just with Cash last night, and I'm in the fucking mood to rub it in bitches' faces. Plus, Bonnie would love to come. She said she was down for the turn up. She didn't mention it on the phone, so I wonder if

Gutta told her anything. If not, she's going to know now," I mentioned.

"Bet. I'm about to go get Brey-bug ready for my momma because Lord knows I do not feel like hearing her mouth today. You know how her old ass can get." Nicki rolled her eyes as she ran upstairs to attend to Aubrey.

I headed straight for the kitchen and grabbed a pack of noodles and popped them in the microwave. I was hungry as hell. I couldn't believe I had stayed all night and morning at this nigga's house, and he didn't feed me shit but dick. I pulled my phone out and decided on texting Cash for the third time. He wasn't replying, and it was really blowing me because what could he possibly be doing that had his attention that much? He was just with me last night and didn't even acknowledge me much. I threw my phone back in my purse.

After eating my noodles, I ran upstairs and hopped in the shower. I threw on a pink, satin set. It came with a spaghetti-strapped T-shirt and a pair of shorts that cut short with a pair of my black fur slides. My shirt came up enough to reveal my belly button, I was so happy I decided on getting this pierced last month. It complemented a lot of my outfits because I always had my stomach showing in almost everything I wore. I was so confident in my body. Yes, I was thirty years old, but my body didn't look like your average thirty-year-old's, and I could thank my momma for that.

I stood an even five-seven with light-caramel skin, deep

cheek dimples, and pretty white teeth to match. My hair was a jet-black color, and it came right above my shoulders. I examined myself in the mirror and applauded myself on how nicely my breasts sat in this shirt. I smiled with triumph and headed downstairs to wait on Nicki so we could head to the salon.

Once we met up with Bonnie, it didn't take us long to get to the hair salon and to get in a chair. I couldn't decide what I wanted, and I didn't feel like trying anything new because we were planning on going to Gutta's party. I didn't feel like looking crazy if I tried some new shit, and it just didn't work out how I expected it to. I swear, every time I tried a new hairstyle, it never came out how I expected it.

"Girl, just get your usual middle-part sew in but have her to add some loose curls. So it'll be different but not too much different," Bonnie said.

"Yeah, that middle-part shit always gon' pop on you," Nicki added. They were right. My middle part was always my go-to because it always worked, and I mean always.

"Yeah, y'all are right. I should get my number one because tonight it's going to be all about us. Damn, I can't wait to see Cash." I licked my lips at the thought of seeing him tonight again.

"Tonight? Um, put me on nobody told me about anything tonight?" Bonnie looked from both of us as she was confused, which I figured she would be like I said before I feel like the only reason Gutta flew her ass out to

Dallas was so she couldn't keep her eyes on him, but she swears he was trying to help her win. I chuckled at the thought of our previous conversation.

"Girl, yes! Tonight, Gutta is having a party, and you didn't know about it, but you be coming at me about Cash? You know Cambria and her little Mexican friend I was telling you about is going to be there, bitch," I said with a bit of sarcasm in my voice. I was always happy to fuck with another bitch's head. Always, and I knew my girls were down for the cause too.

"Girl, you know I don't like Cash, so every chance I get, I'm going to talk shit about his ass, and Gutta probably didn't tell me because he forgot. Y'all know I'm down. I'm going for y'all because I been ready to knock a bitch's head clean off. Especially since bitches out here trying y'all like some lame ass broads. I'm not having it," Bonnie said, facing both of us and making eye contact.

We sat there chatting for a few more moments before we left the salon. I was enjoying this day out with my girls, and tonight was going to be a night to remember. Plotting with my bitches was always fun and brought back great memories. I was ready to give bitches what they've been asking for. They've been sleeping on Henn.

4

Fabio

"I know, Pops. I know. You want me handle that little nigga Marquez, and I told you I would," I said, pulling my hand down my face. My pops had been asking me for almost a week now to make a move on my cousin, and really, I had been bullshitting. Don't get me wrong, I was plotting on his ass since the day my pops first told me he felt like he was trying to snake him, but I was trying to make sure I made the right move before I did anything because my Uncle Gutta wasn't no dumb ass nigga, and Pops knew that, but he didn't give a fuck, and it showed.

"Son, I'm not asking much. I'm just trying to protect our family. His son has been moving on some real fishy shit, and I can't just let it go, 'cause one motherfucker gon' see him doing it and think they can get over too, and before you know it, I'll have the whole city on fire. Therefore, to avoid that, go ahead and handle it tonight at Gutta's all-white party. I won't be there, but I trust you and Cash can get the job done. No hard feelings. It's just when I see someone trying to step on our land and I'm forced to watch them attempt to take from my family's mouth, I got to make a move, and believe me, it's always my best move. Regardless if they ass family or not. You always got to remind niggas that you still on your P's and Q's, and nothing can be taken from you unless you give that shit away. Just hit me back when you have it handled. Oh, and stop fucking on all these little broads and find you a wife, someone like yo' Momma. Love you, son. I'll talk to you sooner than later," Pops said, ending the call.

Every time we got on the phone, he always had a mouthful to say and didn't want to hear anybody's reply. I was pretty used to our conversations by now, especially when he needed a job done. He always kept it short and simple because he knew I could handle anything thrown at me.

On the other hand, he was always trying to pressure me into fucking with just one shorty heavy, but I just wasn't sure I was ready for all that commitment shit just yet. That was nothing new with me though. Well, that was, until I met Josie. That pussy had my head in the clouds, and it was no denying that. Her little, fine ass had a nigga ready to settle down, and I didn't even know shorty last name.

After disconnecting the call with my pops, I took

another pull of my blunt. I had a lot on my plate right now with pops wanting me to step up from just roughing niggas up to actually putting them six feet under, but to put the icing on the cake, he wanted me to kill my cousin. I hit my blunt one more time, trying to relax my mind a bit. I had too much going on.

I guess the reason I was so stressed was because I just didn't know how I could handle all of this at once, and that wasn't like me. I always had a game plan. I knew this blunt would get my mind on the right track. It never failed me. Pops was so ruthless when it came to money. The only people he wouldn't turn on was Moms, Bria, Cash, and myself, and that was literally it. He took Cash in quicker than he did Uncle Gutta, and I never understood the beef between them, but that shit was now surfacing, and everyone was being brought into the middle of it.

I was nothing but grateful that Pops trusted me, considering I wasn't his biological son. My biological pops was back in his country doing God knows what, but I knew it wasn't being a man. He didn't give a fuck about me. He would've kept in touch, but he didn't. Bruce, Cambria's pops, took me in like I was his own, and that meant the world to me. He would always tell me, "any part of your momma is a part of me," and that shit would always stick with me forever. He showed me what a father figure was like, and for that, I'll always look out for him.

Killing was something that came like a second nature to me, so I didn't complain about getting it done. It was just the process of doing it that I needed to prepare myself for. In other words, I was well trained for it, but I was trying to mentally prepare myself for any right or wrong move that could be made. I was already well known and respected in the streets. I say that to say, just like Pops, any move I made had to be my best move. I just didn't know if this—in the streets—was where I could see myself for the rest of my life.

I guess being a street nigga just wasn't for me, because I always wanted to be the father my real pops never was to me. I wasn't the type of nigga that wanted to be in the game long. I wanted to take care of my family, have Aubrey a few little sisters and brothers, and live in a beautiful ass house while the woman of my dreams was feeding me grapes or some shit while the kids were out playing in our big ass backyard. I had a whole plan set out in my head of how I wanted my future to go. I wasn't your ordinary hood nigga. I wanted to be with someone that I could see forever in, someone that I could take care of and pamper without always watching my back, someone that could take care of me and hold shit down like a lady.

I was the most-hated nigga in Atlanta right now, and that was all because of the weight my pops' name held in these streets. Sometimes I wished I wasn't the one with the target on their back or the one that everybody relied on. Sometimes I needed a break from this street shit. I loved it, but they sure as hell didn't love me. Any day could've been my day to meet the good Lord. I'm just lucky that it hadn't been yet. Being the only male in my family, I had more responsibilities than any regular nigga that was my age, but that shit came with the power I deserved.

My phone started ringing again, pulling me from my thoughts. If it was my dad calling back, I was just going to hit ignore. I was going to get the shit handled tonight, and that was gone be the end of that. When I realized it was Nicki, I started to wish it was my father, but instead, I answered the phone. Nicki was my baby momma, but we just couldn't see eye to eye at all. I thought this woman was going to be my wife, but she wasn't who I thought she was when I first met her. I should've known that though considering I picked her ass up from the strip club where she used to work.

"What's up, Nicki? How's my baby girl?" I asked, trying to avoid any bullshit that was about to come out her mouth. I knew if Nicki was calling me, it could only be three things,—she wanted money, dick, or some attention. She always felt the need to tell me about some bullshit that had nothing to do with me at all, like she didn't have her gossiping ass cousin Henn to do that with. I guess that's why her ass was so bitter because I wasn't supplying her ass with neither of the three, and her lonely ass didn't have any real friends that gave a fuck about her. Here lately though she was on some bitter, petty shit more than normal, and it almost had her ass about to be sitting on the blocked list.

That's the main reason I had to cut her off. I didn't have

time for none of the drama that came with her ass, and I found out she wasn't using the money for my daughter like she was supposed to. Instead, her dumbass was gambling it away or trying to keep her and her scamming ass cousin up to par. She didn't know that I knew about her addiction to the casino, but it wasn't hard for me to find out. It wasn't like she was hiding it or anything.

Don't get me wrong, Nicki was a great mother when she wanted to be. She would kill a motherfucker behind Aubrey, and she always made sure my daughter was satisfied, but I sometimes felt like she wasn't doing enough, just the bare minimum to get by or so she wouldn't have me on her ass about how she was supposed to act. One of my biggest pet peeves was telling a woman how to handle her own damn responsibilities. All she wanted to do was find any and every opportunity to hold her hand open, begging me for more money like she couldn't go out and get it on her own, trying to use Aubrey as an excuse.

"Yo' ass answering the phone like you can't check on me and see how I'm doing. Aubrey is fine, of course. Look who her mother is. I mean, I am a whole, full-time single mother out this bitch. Give me some credit," Nicki barked into the phone. So I could already see she was already on some bullshit early this morning, which I wasn't up for. I didn't do negative vibes, which her ass should know by now. She couldn't help it though. Being a crabby ass bitch was something she took a liking to. She loved to argue about nothing.

"Nicki, listen, I'm not up for all that shit today, man, so what is it that you want or need? Before you say money, I want you to know I'm not giving you shit. If Aubrey needs something, I'll come pick her up and take her to get it, but I'm not giving you anything," I replied dryly.

"Bitch, I don't need your money. Like I said, Aubrey straight. I just wanted you to know I heard through the grapevine that yo' ass was booed up with some lil' young bitch at the club last night. Don't be out here embarrassing me. If you gon' fuck with somebody, make sure the bitch is at least half of me. Oh, yeah, and tell your lil' sister if she put her hands on my cousin again behind Cash, I'll lay her little pretty ass out, period. Matter fact, tell that bitch I'll see her tonight!" Nicki spat.

"Now you know better than that. Ain't nobody putting they hands on my little sister without going through me, so I suggest you be on your best behavior, and if you thought the shorty you heard I was with isn't more than you, you could never be more wrong in your life than you are now. Yo' dumbass know for a fact I don't downgrade, and you should know that if you see me with anybody, just know she's more of a woman than you could ever be. Also, she's twenty-five. You're thirty. What you hating for? Now get off my line with those lame ass threats, and don't call me no more unless it's pertaining to my daughter. Bye." I banged on her ass. I just knew she was on some bullshit but not that type of bullshit, worrying about what the fuck I had going on. She should've been past that stage in her life.

My baby girl Aubrey meant the world to me, and I really wanted sole custody of her, but I needed to get my life together first. The courts weren't going to grant me full custody with the life I was living now. That was the main reason I wanted to lay this street shit down. Drug money was the best money, but having a down ass woman on your team that understood you, everything you stood for, and loved you for you that was something I longed for, not this street shit. I think I was big on the whole family man thing because my pops instilled in me to be a family man before anything. I needed to get out my head and go link up with my brother, Cash, to make sure he was straight from last night because he showed his ass as usual.

WHEN I PULLED up to Cash's house, I seen his ex-girlfriend Hennessy's car parked out front, so I just decided to make my way to my sister's house. I was really confused on what he had going on, but I wasn't about to get in the middle of what him and Bria was going through. It wasn't my place or my business. But that nigga just knew he better do right by her. As far as I knew, they weren't on good terms right now, so that nigga could do whatever he wanted to without me beating his ass for it. I don't know why he was fucking with her because he and everybody else knew that fucking with that girl Hennessy wasn't good for his image at all. She was nothing but bad news.

I was glad that I didn't waste my time sitting in the parking lot contemplating on if I should even go to the door because I didn't have time for his ratchet ass ex. If Nicki had something to say about my sister approaching Hennessy in the club, I knew her ass was ready to run her mouth too. But she didn't have all that mouth last night when Bria was right there in front of her ass. Bitches. I laughed.

I just wanted to chill today. I didn't want to have to call Bria to come over here and really beat her ass for disrespecting. I knew my sister could take Henn with her damn eyes closed. These bitches were known for being all bark and no bite, and my sister, on the other hand, never did too much talking, and that was because she was raised to fight, not just run her mouth. I had a lot on my plate. I decided to park in the driveway for a little longer and roll my blunt.

I would just pull up on my sister and chill with her for a bit. Hopefully, I would get to see Jo'. We didn't get to talk much that night at the club before I had to intervene between Cash pistol-whipping some nigga in the middle of the club that Bria was talking to. I tried to tell Cash that every action didn't need a reaction. He was three years younger than me. I was twenty-eight, so I guess you could say he still had a lot of learning to do. I pulled my phone out after I finished rolling my blunt and called my baby sister.

"Hey, sis. Where you at?"

"I'm at home, still trying to get myself together from

last night." Bria yawned into the phone as if I had just woken her from her sleep.

"Yeah, I heard about you knocking Hennessy's ass out last night. I'm about to pull up and chop it up with you. Make sure Jo's fine ass is there." I licked my lips at the thought of her and how I was caressing her body the previous night.

"Boy, she got what she deserved, and that's that. But of course, you know Jo' is going to be here. Where else is she going to be? Don't start trying to use me because you are fucking with her now. Nah, I'm kidding. Just give us a minute to brush our teeth. We aren't getting dressed, because you ain't nobody to impress," Bria said, laughing and ending the call.

My sister was always the type to have a smart-ass mouth. She didn't care how anybody felt about her, looked at her, or anything. She always had to be the center of attention. I assumed that was because she was the only girl, but I wasn't complaining, because I loved her with every bone in my body. Anything she wanted, she got. No questions asked.

I was kind of excited about seeing Jo' again. I wasn't gone cap. She was beautiful as hell. Her vibe was just so much different from other women. I wanted to talk to her because I didn't want her to think that I was trying to take advantage of her.

I was starting to feel bad about the whole situation between me and her because I knew she wasn't that type of female, and I wanted her to know that I understood that, and that shit that happened between us was an accident, and I didn't want her to feel pressured into doing anything she didn't want to do. When I woke up before her, around three a.m. that morning, I decided to leave. I figured it would be best if I wasn't there when she woke up. Not having the chance to explain how I felt about it wasn't doing anything but causing my mind to wonder because I couldn't figure out what was really on her mind.

It didn't take me long to get to my sister's house. She literally stayed ten minutes away from Cash, and sometimes I questioned if they did that on purpose to keep up with each other. My sister and Cash had been messing around for as long as I could remember. They would always pick on each other growing up. When we got in high school, that's when they both agreed that pretending they didn't like each other wasn't doing anything but hurting themselves. But if you ask me, they were better off as friends. Ever since they got together, their relationship has been nothing but craziness, but hey, like I said, that was none of my business. He just needed to do right by her if he didn't want any problems with me. Cash was well respected around my family, so he knew what was expected of him.

"Hey, big head." I walked through Bria's door, trying to spot Jo' until my eyes met with hers as she was walking from her room toward me. Jo' had her hair up in a messy bun, or whatever females called it, like she just hopped out the bed. She was dressed in a white T-shirt that easily revealed her small, round nipples and a pair of gray booty shorts that clung tightly to her ample ass. Although she looked like she had just woke up, she still looked good as fuck. I instantly felt my dick getting hard, but I turned my attention back to my sister.

"Hey, Fabio. How are you?" Jo' said, rubbing sleep from her eyes.

"Hey, lil' mama. I'm straight. What's good with you?" I asked.

"Nothing much. Sorry I look a mess. I wasn't expecting you," Jo' replied, trying to straighten her wrinkled T-shirt out. Little did she know, she had a nigga dick on hard, and she was far from a mess. That natural beauty was always a winner in my book.

"Damn, nigga! Stop undressing my bitch with your eyes, and tell me what you wanted to talk to me about so I can leave y'all two alone to talk." Bria brought my attention back to what I really came to speak with her about.

"Chill. Stop trying to call me out with yo' bobblehead ass. Nicki called me today and said something about you knocking her sister out at the club. What's up with that?" I questioned. I knew my sister was hotheaded, but damn. What could the girl have possibly done for her to knock her ass out cold and then leave her on the bathroom floor? Just ruthless.

"Oh my God! That was the girl you knocked out last night. Fabio, I told her that we shouldn't have left her there, but Bria didn't give a fuck. So of course, I left." Jo' began to spill the beans like no tomorrow.

"Damn, I know who not to do bald-headed hoe shit with." Bria rolled her eyes sarcastically.

"Shut up, bitch. I'm just saying." Jo' rolled her eyes back. I could see she had only been here for a few days, but she was starting to pick up on Bria's ways and adopting some of her own. It wasn't bad though. Having that clap-back was always a plus in a female.

"Y'all, chill the fuck out. Bria, you need to maintain your temper, man. I can't have you out here moving sloppy, dude. You know that."

"First of all, I'm done with this conversation. I'll beat up and knock out whoever the fuck I want to. Instead of preaching to me, you need to be telling them bitches to keep my name out their mouth, or watch who they're stepping to," Bria said, walking away dramatically, heading back to her room. I just laughed as she walked away because Bria was so dramatic, and sometimes, I felt like she did it on purpose.

Jo' walked over to the couch where we were sitting together before and turned the TV on. "Wanna watch a movie?" Jo' asked as she flipped through the Netflix episodes.

"Shit, why not? I did want to talk to you about the other night though. We didn't really get to talk at the club, and I wanted to get this off my chest." I sat down beside her.

"Yeah, I know. I really didn't want to talk about it, but if you insist." Jo's face began to turn red as if she was embarrassed about me even bringing it up. A part of me wanted to know how she felt too because I really wanted to get to know her more, and I didn't want her thinking it was all about the sex. If she was going to fuck with me, communication was something I was big on because that's the only way things would ever work—good communication, and it was no way around that.

"Yeah, I insist because I want to know how you feel about it too. I don't want you to think I just wanted sex, especially with me leaving the other night without even letting you know. I know that made you feel some type of way." I waited for her to respond, and surprisingly she did.

"Honestly, it did make me feel some type of way, but I figured you were just trying to keep it from Bria. You're the first guy I've ever been with... like that, you know?" Did she just say I took her virginity? I knew her shit was tight as fuck, but I just thought it was because she hadn't had sex in a long time, but damn. Taking someone's virginity was something serious.

"I'm a grown man before anything. Whatever I have going on in my relationship or whatever has nothing to do with what I got going on, and I wouldn't dare hide you from anyone ever. So don't think that, and wait... so are you saying I took your virginity?" I asked.

"That sounds good, and yes, you did. Truthfully, I don't regret it one bit. I mean, unless you do." Jo' dropped her head in embarrassment.

"Wait, ma, pick your head up. I can just tell by the way you're acting you aren't that type of female. Believe me when I say your actions make me want you even more. Most females that I've been with have been with way more niggas than me. With you only being twenty-five, that shows me a lot. You have respect for not only yourself, but your body, and that's somebody I can see myself with." I grabbed Jo's chin and placed a kiss on her lips. They tasted like sweet bubblegum as our tongues danced around in each other's mouths.

"You know, I've never ever had a boyfriend before, so I don't know how this is supposed to go." Jo' pulled away from our kiss and was now looking me in my eyes. I sat for a second contemplating on what she had just said. I was trying to ask God if He really sent this woman for me or what.

"Just be yourself. Let niggas know if they try you, that you're mine. That won't be hard for them to find out. But we can take things slow. I don't want you to seem like you're rushing anything. So for now, you're my shorty," I told her.

Josie was really a different type of breed, and that shit was so rare. Not many bitches around here her age even still had their virginity. Most women I fucked with didn't even have it. I was looking forward to getting to know Josie more, and I could definitely see myself being with her. She was so cute and shy, and that shit just made me want her even more. My only concern was would she be able to keep up with a nigga like me.

I kissed her goodbye and told her and my sister I looked forward to seeing them tonight at my uncle Gutta's party. Sad to say, tonight on his birthday, he was about to lose his only son. This was the only chance I had to make my move with it being least expected, and I knew tonight being accomplished would make Pops proud. So I had to do what I had to do. I just hoped Josie stayed out the way and wasn't a witness of this side of me.

"You know we'll be there looking pretty. Uncle Gutta gon' have some buttaheads there, so we have to be there to make shit pop with our pretty asses," Cambria said, returning from upstairs fully dressed.

"Don't be out there acting stupid. Hate to have to beat a motherfucker up behind y'all asses because you know I will, Bria," I reminded her.

"Shut up, Fab. You aren't going to shoot your homie Cash. If that's the case, you would've been did it. Just make sure that nigga stay out my way tonight. Please, brother. Now I don't mean any harm, but we have a lot to do. Don't you have to meet up with Cash or something?" Bria's slick ass replied as I pulled Jo' in for a kiss. I did have some shit to handle though.

One thing about my sister was she always had a comeback for anything. She was right though. I needed to get out of there so I could put shit in motion with Cash. He would be helping me on this mission anyway. If there was one person I knew I could always depend on, it was Cash. He always came through.

My father wanting me to kill my cousin tonight at my uncle Gutta's birthday party was some tough shit. I loved my cousin to death, but once you crossed my pops, you had crossed me. Tonight, was my uncle Gutta's all-white party, and he had damn near invited the whole neighborhood. Pops knew it was a chance that Gutta would find out, but he wanted this to be a warning. This was just going to be a night that everyone was going to remember.

5

Josie "Jo"

Having that talk with Fab really cleared things up for me. I'm sure it was more things I could learn about him that could possibly impact me as well with what he did as a living, but something was telling me it was worth giving him a chance. I know we started off on a foot that I probably wouldn't started off with anybody else, but it didn't seem to make the vibe between us any different like I thought it would. The only difference now was I was sober, and he had my emotions at an all-time high. The way he held my chin, looked me in my eyes, and kissed me made me feel like he really meant everything he said.

Fab hadn't given me any reason that I shouldn't have believed everything he had said to me, so I was giving him the benefit of the doubt. I was actually happy that he wanted to take things slow because that was my only requirement. I didn't know that Cambria introducing me to him would have me crushing for his ass so soon. Everything about Fab was different, down to his swag. No, I hadn't had a boyfriend before, but I knew what I wanted in a man, and one that could keep it straight with me was one that I wanted on my team forever because men like that were rare.

"Get out of your feelings. Let's go get our nails done or something. We can find our outfits when we get back," Bria said, dragging me from my thoughts.

"Alright. Let me freshen up, and I'll be back so we can go." I walked up the steps and headed straight for the shower. I didn't stay in long because I didn't want to keep Bria waiting. I stepped into a pink jumpsuit with a pair of black Nikes and was ready for the day. I noticed that being around Fab didn't allow my mind any room to think about what happened to my family, and I liked that. I didn't want to think about the negative all the time.

When we arrived at the nail salon, I didn't even know what to think or expect. Bria said she would help me pick out a style, and I was completely fine with that. We sat in these big, lounge chairs getting our nails done first, and then we headed to the pedicure bowl to get our feet done.

"So best, have you ever had a wax before?" Bria asked, breaking the silence.

"No, I haven't. Not yet of course. What about you?" I chuckled as the nail tech scrubbed the bottom of my feet.

"Yes, I get them all the time. We should get one together. Today!" Bria said.

"Sure, why not? I mean, what could it hurt?" I asked.

"Girl, not a damn thang. That wax gon' have that little kitty looking like a glazed honey bun," Bria said as we both fell out in laughter.

Our nails and feet were done in no time. I got yellow while Bria got white. Yellow was my favorite color, so of course, that was my first option. I could get used to this. I loved being girly and looking good. With this new life I was living, there was no doubt I was going back any time soon.

THE TIME FLEW BY TODAY. Before I knew it, it was time for us to get ready for the party. It was an all-white party, and I was ready to slip in this two-piece set that Bria had got for me when we were at the mall. It was a halter-top piece with a pair of white pants that hugged my hips like no tomorrow. I decided on wearing a pair of red bottoms to complete my outfit. My hair was styled bone straight with a middle part in the center of my head. I had never worn my hair like that before, always ponytails, because I didn't have a need to do it really, but Bria thought this would be different. I liked it because I didn't look so young, and I know I said I wouldn't, but I agreed on letting Bria do my makeup tonight simply because I loved how I looked going to the club the previous night Fab couldn't keep his hands off of me. I was kind of upset our night got ruined with Bria and Cash's shenanigans, but hey, when best-friend duties call, they call.

Bria had so many talents when it came to fashion that I was sometimes questioning why she didn't go to school for it. Bria was just a wild person. She didn't even seem like the type that would go to college. But it was still the thought that counted. I walked downstairs, letting Bria examine me from head to toe before we jumped in the back of the Uber.

I was glad I brought my gold clutch tonight because something was telling me to grab my taser that Bria had bought me. Ever since the last club incident, I didn't want to be that friend that was lacking at any point and time, because I could already see now that being friends with Bria came with hating ass bitches that you didn't even know. I didn't mind that though, because also being friends with Bria taught me how to stand up for myself. These bitches in the States were a different breed from what I'm used to.

"Tonight is going to be so much fun, best friend. I'm not going to start no shit with anybody, as long as bitches don't start with me. Meaning, Cash better stay his ass far away from me as possible if he knows what's good for him," Bria said, flashing her tiny, pink 9mm.

"What are you going to do with that?" My eyes got big because I didn't even know Bria had a gun.

"Nothing, as long as nobody messes with you or me. Now, let's go, best." Bria climbed out of the car, and I could hear the loud music playing from the inside of the mansion.

"Wow, this is nice." I followed close behind Bria so I wouldn't get lost.

"I see y'all made it," Fab said, grabbing me around my waist from behind. He lucky I recognized his voice because I was ready to go off.

"Of course. Why wouldn't we?" I said in a flirtatious way. Fab was looking good as fuck. He had on a pair of white Balmain pants with a fresh ass. white Polo T-shirt. His gold accessories matched him so well. I didn't even realize he had his gun on his hip until I looked down. I didn't know what he had it for, nor did I know what he did for a living, but I knew whatever it was, Fab and his sister felt like they needed to protect themselves at all times, and I didn't see anything wrong with that.

"Listen, I got something to handle, so I want y'all to stay out the way and just try to enjoy yourselves. I'll make sure I link back up with y'all after the party. A'ight?" Fab said, looking from me and Bria.

"Don't do nothing stupid, Fab. Seriously. This is Gutta's birthday bash."

"I got this. Mind yours. I'll catch y'all later." Fab planted a kiss on my cheek before he disappeared in the crowd. I didn't know what he had in mind, but I wasn't worried about all of that. I was curious as to why it was three bitches staring at me and Bria from across the living room. I didn't say anything about the girls. I just turned my attention away from them. Maybe they thought we were cute. Bria took me to the other side of the room, near the kitchen, where she introduced me to her Uncle Gutta.

"What's good, niece? I'm glad you could make it, and who's this pretty lady you brought with you? I haven't seen her around before." Gutta licked his lips as he was undressing me with his eyes. He was starting to make me feel uncomfortable, so I just looked away.

"This is my best friend, Jo'. She's from Brazil, so of course you wouldn't have seen her around, but you will now." Bria wasn't even paying attention at how her uncle was eyeing me. Of course she didn't say anything, because if she did, she would've been on his ass. I didn't want to ruin anything, so I just brushed it off. Maybe that's how he was with everybody.

"I look forward to that, but where is your brother at? I saw him for a split second earlier, and that was it."

"I'm not sure, but here, let's turn up! It's your day, nigga!" Bria handed him a double shot of Patrón and passed me one. I immediately threw it back. I wasn't trying to feel so awkward around him anymore, and I knew the liquor was going to do just that.

Her uncle wasn't a bad-looking guy. You could tell he was older than us but not too old. He had smoke-gray hair, where some parts were lighter than others. His skin was a creamy- caramel color. He looked like the type that could bag any female he wanted regardless of age, so why the hell was he staring at me so hard? His broad shoulders and tatted arms gave off the impression that he did some time in the feds or that he was just really good about lifting weights every day. My attention was pulled away from his looks when some random girl walked up.

"Hey, Gutta. How are you?" one of the girls that was with the group staring at us said, approaching Gutta.

"What's up, lil' mama? You know today my birthday. You want to give me a lap dance, shorty?" Gutta said as he took a pull on his blunt.

"Of course I do." The girl grabbed his hand and pulled him to the closest couch, being sure we saw her every move.

"Ugh, this little, dirty bitch is back from the slums." Bria rolled her eyes and raised her glass to her mouth again.

"You know her? I didn't want to say anything, but she was with a group of girls that was staring at us earlier," I finally admitted.

"Yeah, probably her weird ass best friend and her cousin, Nicki. You remember the bitch I dropped in the club the other night? That's her best friend, Bonnie, and those bitches try to be relevant so bad it's sad." Bria grabbed my hand and pulled me upstairs to this room.

"Wait, so they followed us here?" I was curious as to how they even knew about the party, and if they knew Bria didn't like them, why in the hell were they here.

"Girl, they probably saw a flyer somewhere and took that as their opportunity to be seen. I came up here so I could clear my mind before I start airing this bitch out. I said I was going to be on my best behavior, but I can't stand when bitches try me like a punk." Bria pulled a small baggy from her purse and popped a pill in her mouth.

"What's that?" I questioned. I had never seen Bria take pills before, but I could tell this was something new. She was going through some shit, and I was starting to feel bad about not even talking to her about it.

I was the type of person that wanted the person to come to me first if they really wanted to talk, but I guess that wasn't good, so I made a promise to myself that I would talk to her when we got alone together the next time. I couldn't have my best friend out here going crazy behind these niggas, especially Cash. He wasn't it. In my opinion anyway.

"Nothing, just birth control. Don't want to slip up and get pregnant." Bria gave me a weak smile.

"Whatever you say. We're going to talk tonight because I need you to get out whatever you're holding in. You act like you don't have feelings, but bitch, me of all people, you know I know you." I was impressed how I just handled that situation. Cambria was rubbing off on me more than I thought she was.

"Yeah, OK. Anyway, just because bitches eyeing us like it's a problem don't mean nobody scared. I'm waiting on bitches to make a move. Bonnie stank ass think shit sweet just because my uncle let her give his stupid ass a lap dance. I really don't know what she hyped about. He'll let a crackhead dance on him if she was thick. I'll be sure to let them bitter bitches see me leave with Cash and you with Fab. Period." Bria's eyes where now low and glossy, and I could tell she was ready to get on her bullshit. At this point, it didn't even matter. I was on whatever my best friend was on. I saw now that hanging with Bria, I had to be ready to do bald-headed hoe shit whenever she was ready, as she would say.

"I'm with whatever you on, best friend. Let's go show these bitches who they really fucking with," I replied as I felt the sober me now escaping my body. I wasn't a big alcohol fan, so that little double shot had me feeling myself.

"There goes my bitch!" Bria looked at me and grabbed my hand to follow behind her. As soon as we stepped foot out of the bedroom, we heard a gunfire.

Pow! Pow! Pow!

"What the fuck is going on?" I screamed. Bria pulled me back into the room and pulled her phone out.

"Fab? You good? What's going on down there? Jo' and I are stuck upstairs." Bria waited for a moment to respond, and I assumed Fab was telling her what to do.

"Alright, Jo', we're about to go out the back door. It's a room up here that has an elevator, and it'll take us down to the garage where we're going to meet Fab and Cash. I don't know what's going on, but I hope one of those bullets hit

Hennessy." Bria laughed, but I knew she was being serious.

The sound of the gunshots brought back memories of when I was in Brazil and my family was being murdered. Tears began to flow down my cheeks, and I tried to wipe them away. I just ran with Bria's hand in mine until we got down to the basement. I knew my makeup was a mess, and I didn't want Fab to see me like that.

"Noooo! Marquez! What the fuck happened?" Bria yelled, and she let out a loud shrill, forcing me to open my eyes. I stood there for a minute as I watched the blood leak from his head, making a mess on the concrete. I was frozen, and I couldn't move. Just how I was when my family was being assassinated one by one while I hid under the cabinets of our bathroom.

"Come on, ma. Don't cry. Everything is going to be alright. Here, sit right here." Fab lifted me up in the back seat of an all-black Tesla while Bria got in on the other side. She held my hand the whole way to our destination.

"Fab, what happened back there, man, and don't lie to me?" Bria asked with concern in her voice. I had never met her cousin before, but I could tell she cared for him by the way she was acting. I had never seen her so vulnerable until now.

"Baby, it's alright. We will talk about it when we get to my house," Cash answered for Fab. He was sitting in the passenger seat now turned around facing Bria.

"Shut the fuck up! I just want to know now what

happened, so don't bullshit me. Tell me right now! Or I'm calling Daddy!" Bria screamed through tears, sounding childlike, causing a scene in the back seat. I just sat in silence because I still didn't know how to feel. I was starting to regret even coming out tonight. If I knew it was going to be the part two of Brazil all over again, I wouldn't have agreed on coming out. I didn't even know Gutta anyway, and by the way he was making me feel, I didn't want to know him either.

"You know what, Bria? That might be your best bet to call Pops and see what really happened." Fab sounded like he was more aggravated than anything. He kept his attention on the road with his face remaining stern, showing no emotion.

I watched as Bria covered her mouth in disbelief. "Don't tell me Daddy had something to do with Marquez being killed. Our own fucking family!"

"Like I said, call Pops, and see what's up," Fabio said and then turned the radio up to drown out Bria's questioning.

I was so confused. Did Fab and Cash have something to do with his death? It was Gutta's birthday. Why today of all days if so? I was so confused and trying to put two and two together, but I kept coming up with nothing. Bria and I were only upstairs for ten minutes at the most, so what could've transpired that quickly? When we pulled up to the Hyatt, I was perplexed on why we were here.

"Fab, take me the fuck home! I don't want to be around

y'all right now!" Bria cried. Now that we were in the light, I could see that she had been crying.

"This ain't the time to be acting like a baby. I don't care what you want. You're going to get your ass out this car, go check into this room, and stay with Cash, and Jo' is going to stay with me. We'll be in the same suite. I just need to keep my eyes on y'all tonight. I'm not taking no for an answer, so get your ass out of the truck," Fab said, looking Bria dead in her eyes. She did exactly what was asked of her. I was surprised she didn't put up a fight, but I guess she knew what was best for her. I had so many questions to ask Fab, and I was going to get to the bottom of this. I needed to know what was going on. I felt so behind.

6

Fabio "Fab"

I felt so bad about putting the girls in that situation. But killing that nigga as soon as I laid eyes on him was at the very top of my list. Shit wasn't supposed to be as messy as it was, but shit, I got the job done. As soon as the mission was complete, I called my pops and let him know that the job had been done. He knew it was a chance that my uncle Gutta would've found out, but he didn't give a fuck. My pops was the most ruthless nigga I ever came across. I felt bad for putting Jo' and Bria in the middle of that, but I didn't feel bad about doing what I had to do to protect my family's money.

In my book, they were my blood, and that was what I was raised to protect. I just hoped the situation didn't make Jo' look at me any different. I really fucked with shorty, and I could see us getting somewhere, but I might've fucked up any chance of that I had with that bullshit. I should've waited until she left or something, but I just couldn't. Once it was set in my head to get a job done, that's what I was going to do. Being trigger happy was my biggest flaw. I made the decision of getting a room so we could all stay together. I just needed to know they were going to be safe tonight.

We finally arrived and checked into the suite, which had two adjacent bedrooms, which gave us plenty of space from each other. I picked a hotel that was completely off the grid. My homeboy, Carlos, owned it, and he always threw me a room when I really needed it if I threw him some work. It was a fair trade if you ask me.

I really wanted to get some alone time with Jo' so I could see what was really running through her head about the type of nigga she thought I was. I knew Cash and Bria had some unfinished business, and I didn't mind letting them hash things out while I kicked it with Jo'. Seeing her cry in the back seat of my Tesla did something to a nigga. I usually didn't do that soft shit, but it was different with her.

Bria wasn't talking to me, so I'm sure she was happy to not be sharing the same room with me. She didn't even tell me good night. I didn't stress it though. In due time, Bria would understand that what I did was to protect her and the family.

Bria was still new to the game, and she wasn't with all the shit I was with, but she had it in her. I felt like she tried so hard to push that hood up out of her, but she just couldn't. She even went away to college to start a new life was what she called it, but she came back home when she finally figured out it wasn't for her. So just like this, her being upset with me isn't the right thing to do right now, but she'd come around, and I wasn't pressing no issues.

When we entered the suite, I wasted no time apologizing to Jo' because she deserved that. I barely got to know her and was already introducing her to this street life, and I just wanted us to start off on a good foot.

"Listen, Jo', I'm sorry for the shit you had to witness tonight," I said, breaking the silence. She was sitting on the edge of the bed, just looking out the window as if she was stuck in a daze.

"I know, Fab. I'm not mad at you. It just brought back a lot of memories that I didn't plan on sharing so soon, but you know, things happen, and this might be a good thing that I'm sharing this with someone besides Bria. I mean, I really didn't ever want to bring it up, nor did I want it to have any effect on our relationship, because I don't come from the prettiest background." Jo' looked at me with tears in her eyes, and I could tell whatever she had been holding in was some deep shit.

"Lil' mama, I'm far from judging anybody. That isn't even some shit I involve myself in. I have no room to judge someone off their past. I mean, look at what I do," I admitted.

"It's just so hard talking about this. My family was very poor when I lived in Brazil. Yeah, we had our own store, but we didn't make much money. My parents had to do what they could to keep the bills paid. My dad started working for the cartel in Brazil, and he put our family in jeopardy to be killed. I came here because I wanted to start fresh. The cartel may still be searching for me, but I happened to get away. Every day, I'm forced to see my family's faces of how they were left for dead, and it hurts. I just want to forget it all. I know that will never happen, but it's a wish I long to have come true. Tonight just brought back too many memories." Jo' was now laying her head on my shoulder, and I could feel the tears seeping through my white T-shirt. This shit was deeper than I thought it would be.

Seeing her like this was making me feel more worse about the situation. I didn't know that she had been through that shit. Bria didn't tell me anything about it, but I assumed that was because it wasn't her place to tell. I pulled Jo' close to me and held her because that's what she needed right now, and I wanted to reassure her that as long as I was around, she was always going to be in good hands.

"Jo', as long as I'm around, you won't ever have to feel scared again. You can walk anywhere you want comfortably. I can bet that. I'm going to protect you with everything in me. Man, that's some deep shit, and that made me want to go even harder for you. You deserve the best of the best. Ain't shit wrong with growing up broke as long as you find a way to come out on top, and you did. Tonight was a big mistake. I hope it didn't make you look at me any different. I really wanted to get to spend this time with you so we could get to know each other better." I revealed.

"Of course not, Fab. I could never look at you different from that. I'm sure you had a good reason for doing what you did. I'm just thankful you aren't looking at me crazy because of what I came from and how I ended up here. Believe me when I say I am very family oriented, and family means the most to me, but something wanted me to protect myself. I feel like I can do our name justice." Jo' fed me her logic of the whole situation.

I wasn't in no shape to judge this woman. Her sharing this information with me just made me want to be there for her even more. Honestly, I probably would've did the same shit. I didn't know what she was going through in that country, and I couldn't even imagine.

Although I had just met shorty, it was something in me that only wanted to make sure she was straight. I let out a huff because I now knew that I made a big mistake. She looked up at me and kissed me, and I kissed shorty back but not on no hardcore ass shit. It was like we were making love but with our tongues. I wasn't going to cap. Jo' was bad as fuck, and it was no denying that. I just wanted to please her.

I laid her back on the bed, undressing her with my teeth. This time, her body was more relaxed than it was the first time we had sex. The way her honeypot dripped, I knew she wanted it as bad as I did. I licked my lips as she gasped and moaned to the drum of my thumb against her clit. She sounds of her purr only made my dick grow harder.

Everything about this woman turned me on. She could throw me a small smile, and I'd probably bust all over myself. Oddly, no woman had ever had that effect on me ever. It was so different being with her. It was easy and peaceful. She had to be the one.

I unzipped my pants and asked permission before entering inside of her water gates. "May I?" I whispered in her ear as she gently bit down on her bottom lip.

"Please," Jo' moaned softly as I continued to dance with my thumb up and down her opening. I stuck my thumb in my mouth to taste her sweet juices.

"I'm going to take my time with this pussy this time," I moaned softly in her ear. I pulled her panties off with my teeth and twirled my tongue around in her sweetness. She tugged on my dreads as I went deeper inside of her. Jo's legs began to shake, and her moaning turned into soft yelps. I could tell she was about to cum, and I didn't want to move.

"Shit. Bab—" I cut Jo's sentence off with a passionate kiss as I entered inside of her with my shaft. I gyrated to the beat of her moans as I penetrated her G-shot with each stroke. I wasn't even fucking her no more. I was making love to shorty, and this feeling was unexplainable.

"Baby girl, do you forgive me?" I questioned as I deepened myself inside of her.

"Yes, daddy. I do. I forgive you," Jo' uttered.

As soon as I felt her about to climax, I pulled out and picked her up and sat her on my dick. We were chest to chest as she grinded on me like I was a stripper pole. My toes curled with each hip roll as she creamed all over my dick. It made me go wild, and I busted inside of her. I fell back on the bed butter-ball ass naked.

Normally, after I fucked someone, I would've been up and out the door. It wasn't even that type of party with her. I actually wanted to cuddle with shorty. We lay together until she fell asleep. We didn't finally get to bed until around three a.m. I just lay there until the sun came up, admiring how beautiful she was. I just never knew there was a feeling that made a nigga feel the way I did about Jo'. This shit was indescribable. Lying next to her was the only place I wanted to be, especially after all of the bullshit that happened today.

~

Once the girls woke up, me and Cash had to go meet with Pops, so we dropped them off at their spot. Cash and Bria seemed like they were on good terms because when we dropped them off, they kissed each other goodbye. As bad as they drove each other nuts, I felt like they were perfect for each other. Hennessy, his ex-girlfriend, was just a waste of time, but she wasn't going anywhere unless Cash made her, and believe me, that's the moment everybody was waiting for.

"Bro, I really love Bria, man. Seeing her tore up like that and all in her feelings did something to me, man. I got to do right by her. She deserves that."

"You know, not even on no soft shit, I was feeling the same way about Jo'," I said, keeping the conversation to a minimum and my eyes on the road. I wasn't trying to get too off topic because I knew this meeting with Pops was going to be intense.

I hadn't heard from my uncle at all last night, and my mind couldn't help but wonder what his next move was going to be. Gutta used to run the streets until my pops stepped in and started making more moves than him. My pops pretty much ran this city and everyone that lived in it. My uncle became a worker for my dad a while back, and ever since he fell into that role, it was like he just couldn't deal with my dad being younger than him and being his boss at the same time.

The way my uncle acted, you could always tell that he needed recognition in anything he did. This man could go to the store or handle a nigga like he was supposed to, and he would expect a pat on the back. He always tried to equal Marquez up to me and always try to compare us. I knew my dad was going to start noticing that and falling back from him. My dad never included Uncle Gutta's son in anything we did because he knew he wouldn't be trustworthy. That's why Pops left it up to me to pick my partner in crime. He knew I thought just like him, so I knew who the right and wrong person was to be in my circle.

"Yeah, bro, last night really opened my eyes to a lot of shit. I can't lose Bria for nothing, man. That girl is my whole world," Cash said, breaking the silence.

All I could do was agree with him in silence because I couldn't shake my head from what we were up against. My uncle Gutta wasn't my pops, but he did have connections, and he knew a lot of what we were capable of, so that made us an easy target for him. When we arrived at my moms and pops' house, I was a little bit more at ease. Being at their house always brought me peace, especially when mom was in.

"Hey, baby. How have you been?" my mom said, kissing me on the forehead. She hadn't seen me in a few months because she was in another country getting things in order.

My mom was a busy woman, and she always stayed with something to do. She was in the kitchen cooking Pops some dinner, I assumed, by the aroma of pot roast coming from the crock pot.

"I'm fine, Ma. I've missed you. How was your trip?" I questioned. She knew I didn't fuck with the type of work she did. My mom was out here having babies for people and getting paid hella bread. I just didn't feel comfortable with her putting her body through that, especially since she was getting older.

My pops would tell my mom all the time that she didn't have to work, but my mom wasn't a dependent ass woman. She did things by herself, and she was going to continue to do that until she laid to rest. Although I hated her hustle, I respected it on so many levels.

"I've missed you too, baby. You know business is business. Don't worry your pretty, little head about it. Your dad is upstairs in his office waiting on you. When y'all come back down, I'll have you guys some of this dinner I made. Y'all look like shit, and Cash, don't be coming in my house acting like you can't speak," my mom said, laughing. She was always straightforward and didn't care how it sounded or how it came out. She was always going to say what was on her mind.

"I'm sorry, Mrs. Wilson. I was too hypnotized by that smell of that macaroni and cheese you have over there," Cash said, rubbing his stomach.

"Yeah, I bet." My mom turned back to the kitchen to finish what she was doing. I knew that was our key to gone about our business.

I'm sure we did look crazy, though we had a long ass night, and then after that night I had with Jo', her little ass had me not giving a fuck about what anybody else thought about me. As long as I looked good to her, it was straight.

I barely got any sleep, and I could bet money that I was going to be missing out on sleep for a few days trying to get shit handled with my little cousin Marquez's death.

"A'ight, Mom, see you in a bit," I said as Cash followed me upstairs. My pops was sitting behind his desk with a case of cigars sitting on his desk.

"Well, well, here is my men that can accomplish anything they're up against. Y'all young niggas have made me so proud here. Sit down. Let's smoke a cigar. Tell me was last night too much for y'all?" Pops inquired as he handed us both a cigar.

I sat back in my chair and took advantage of this time to relax my mind. I didn't really like cigars, but this shit had a nigga really feeling like a young, rich nigga. "Pops, last night was crazy, but nothing is never too much to a giant," I replied confidently.

"Bruce, like Fab said, you know there is no job too big for us. We get shit done, and that's the end of that. You know how we come behind this family name. I'll never have nothing but the utmost respect for you because you took me in like your own son and never made me feel no different. Whatever you need, I got you. Facts," Cash said, taking a pull of his cigar and laying his head back on the chair as if he was relaxing.

"I couldn't have picked a better duo to run these streets for me. I do want y'all to know that this isn't the end. The battle has just begun. Gutta was blowing me up last night and the early hours of the morning trying to blame his son's death on me. It was my fault, and I'm not knocking that I did set the hit, but I know he isn't going to live this down," Pops said, pulling his fully-ringed hand down his face. Pops never went without his jewelry on. If you ever seen him without it, just know something wasn't right.

The crazy thing about it was Pops went anywhere comfortably, no matter how many people he crossed. His money was always good just like his face card. People just knew not to cross him ever, so when I found out about my cousin trying to sneak and do snake shit, that shit surprised me because he, of all people, knew how this shit could go.

"Wait, so I hope you don't want us to kill Gutta'?" I questioned.

"No, no, no, y'all won't have any parts in that. He is my battle, which I'll need to handle on my own. I'll keep y'all in the loop though. Here's a few bands. Go buy yourselves something nice, take a trip, or something. Y'all deserve it," Pops said, handing us each a stack of money.

I smiled because the only thing I loved about the work I did was that I got paid better than any general job was out here paying. We left Pops' office and let him get back to plotting his ideas on killing Gutta. My job was done, and I had nothing else to worry about. At least that's what I thought.

7

Fabio "Fab"

Leaving Pops' crib, I felt like a weight was lifted off my shoulders. Although the games had just begun, I wasn't worried about shit. Jo' and I were in a great place right now, and my pockets were full. I couldn't complain even if I wanted to.

"So what you think about a trip to Cancun with the girls? I mean, I know you and Jo' just started rocking, but I can see you really feelings shorty. I haven't seen you fuck with one shorty since the night we chilled at Bria's and you met Jo'." Cash turned the music down, and now he had my full attention when he mentioned a trip. After last night, that's really what we all needed.

"You know what, bro? That don't even sound bad. That'll not only give us a break from the city, but that'll give me more time to get to know Jo'. She told me some shit last night, bro, that really fucked me up because I wasn't expecting her to react the way she did," I said, now pulling into my driveway. To my surprise, when I pulled in, I saw my baby mother standing on my porch with my daughter in her hand.

"What the hell could she possibly want? Just when the day was going somewhat good, her come her stupid ass," I said, pulling my hand down my irritated face.

"Bro, out of all of the bitches in the world, why did you get Nicki pregnant?" Cash asked with a serious look on his face.

"Nigga, I was caught up in the moment. This wasn't really supposed to happen the way it did. But it did. I couldn't stop it," I admitted.

Nicki was originally just some chick I was hooking up with from time to time more than I was anybody else, and when she popped up pregnant, I thought of asking her to get an abortion, but I couldn't do that. I started thinking about the child and how he or she didn't even ask to be here. So I did what I was supposed to do and stepped up to the plate like the man my pops raised me to be. The blessing I got out of my baby girl was more than a nigga could ever ask for, but it was just irritating that I had her mother attached to the picture.

"Nigga, I'm telling you Aubrey is a blessing, but I wasn't having that shit with Henn's ass. She knew I didn't want no kids with her dumb ass, but she constantly let me bust all in her dumb ass. Now I know this might sound bad, but the girl I really want is Bria, and I don't care what I have to do, but I'm going to prove myself to her."

"Cash, you better, nigga, because I'm not just going to sit around and watch you hurt my sister, because she doesn't deserve that. As far as the abortion thing, I could never do that. You a bold one, my nigga. But look, you might have some shit going on today too. Look who just hopped out the passenger side of Nicki's car." I pointed to Henn. She stood there with her arms crossed like this was the moment she had been waiting for.

"Nah, I'm 'bout to shut this shit down," Cash said as he climbed out the car.

"Get your ass out the car, Fab! I'm so sick of your shit. I saw you leave the club with that little ass girl last night." Nicki switched a crying Aubrey from one hip to another. I didn't like all this attention in front of my crib. The only reason her ratchet ass knew where I stayed was because she had my daughter, and you never knew what could happen.

"Yo, watch your mouth in front of my daughter, man. I don't have shit to prove to you, Nicki. We aren't together anymore." I grabbed my daughter from her ass and kissed her.

"I don't have to watch shit! This my motherfucking mouth, my motherfucking baby, and nobody is going to beat my motherfucking ass! Now, tell me what's up with you and that little ass girl!" Nicki questioned.

I stood there for a second because I couldn't believe this was the mother of my firstborn. I knew that sooner or later I would have to share this information with Jo', but I didn't want to push her away. I wasn't worried about Bria saying anything, because she never meddled in my business, but Nicki? Nicki, on the other hand, was going to make it her business.

"If I tell you, will you just leave me the fuck alone unless it pertains to my daughter, and will you promise to never go near her? I saw you eyeing her at my uncle Gutta's birthday bash, but I didn't have time to come check your ass." I looked back and saw Cash and Henn going back and forth. Cash was standing there like he gave no fucks in the world, and I'm more than sure that was the case. It was crazy how you'd show a female that you didn't want them, and they still came around acting delusional as hell. I didn't know how many times I would run into Nicki again, but I knew her ass wasn't going to let it rest, especially after she found out I was fucking with Jo' on some potential-relationship type shit. But hopefully, she would give me enough time to tell her first.

"Yeah, yeah, yeah, I promise. Now tell me nigga." Nicki flipped her hair from one shoulder to the other and then crossed her arms again.

"Yeah, I'm fucking with her and on some heavy shit, so I don't need you interfering. You really think just because you're my baby momma you can do whatever you want to do, but all that shit dead. You know I'm not no lame ass nigga, so please don't push me to do some shit I don't want to do." I threatened, but I meant every word I meant. I just wanted her to understand how serious I was.

"Whatever, Fab. You won't have my baby around that bitch."

"She doesn't even know I have a child yet, but when she does find out, I'll have her around anybody I want to. She's my daughter just as much as she's yours," I replied.

"Oh, so you out here flaunting this bitch around, but you haven't told her you have a fucking kid? Oh, that's real fucking low. Now that you mentioned that, I just might talk to her ass." Nicki spat. I felt Aubrey's body becoming heavier and heavier in my arms, and I could tell she had fallen asleep.

"Hold that thought. Let me go lay my daughter down." I went to Nicki's car and laid her back down on the back seat. Cash was now walking into the house, and Henn was sitting in her front seat of the car crying like she had just found out the worst news in her life.

I couldn't wait to hear what Cash had to say to her. I just wished Nicki would get it. She always had to make shit difficult. She was really trying me like I wouldn't have her ass touched for interfering with my personal life, but I was capable of all things. She knew that. I just hated when I had something good going for myself, somebody always tried to come along and fuck up my happiness. I wasn't having it that time. I grabbed Nicki by her arm and pulled her inside because the last thing I needed was my neighbors in my business.

"Nicki, I'm not going to give you too many more warnings. If you go anywhere near Jo', I'll lay your ass out and raise my beautiful daughter by myself, and you know I have no problem with that." I had my hands around her neck but not as tight as I wanted them to be.

"Nigga, please! You don't scare nobody. You can't even get custody of Aubrey if you wanted to, and we all know that. Isn't that right, Cash?" Nicki made sure to look past me and make eye contact with Cash.

"Bitch, leave me out of it." Cash sat down on the couch and turned the television on to watch the current game.

"Don't you ever disrespect me. If I can't get custody of her, my parents can. Please believe me when I say this isn't a game you want to play. You saw that body that dropped last night? It could've easily been you." I let that slip out my mouth before I could stop it. Nicki just did something to me. She always knew a way to piss me off or to push me to that point. Before I could even realize it, I had her neck gripped tightly between my hands. Her color started to leave her face and replace with blue. I let my grip go, and she fell limp to her knees.

"Don't you ever, in your life, put your hands on me again. I can't believe that bitch got you out here wilding like that. But it's all good. I'm leaving, but this won't be the last you see of me! Oh, yeah, you won't be seeing Aubrey either until you stop seeing that bitch. Now, bye!" Nicki slammed my door as she walked out. I didn't even give a fuck. I just wanted her to feel where I was coming from. Now that I said something about Marquez, I felt like she was going to try to use that against me as much as she possibly could. How she was going to do that, I didn't know, but I had a trip to plan with Cash and the girls.

8

Uncle Gutta

I really couldn't believe my own brother had my son killed. I was so tired of running these streets for that nigga. I swear I was. This drug-lord shit was supposed to be handed down to me, but my pops gave it to my brother, Bruce, instead. I was always the one to get the shorter end of the stick out of us two. Although I was the oldest, my father seen more potential in my baby brother than me. In reality, I've been in these streets longer and knew way more shit than Bruce.

Growing up, I would always keep him out of shit and try to show him the opposite path of this street shit because he wasn't built for this shit, but what do you know? My dad trained his ass up right. Well, in his book, it would be a pat on the fucking back for killing his own blood. I'd never forget when my own pops had his only blood sister killed because she owed him some money. My aunt Tammy had been in some debt with my dad for a while. I'd never forget the day I came home from school, and my mom was sitting in the kitchen floor holding my aunt's lifeless body in her arms as she cried. I could never shake that image.

After that, I think it changed my relationship with my father. I'd never been the type to switch up on my own blood. That may be the real reason my dad picked my little brother over me, but it damn sure wasn't a good one, because the chaos my baby brother was causing had his ass in for a rude awakening because back then, I didn't have it in me to kill my own blood, but now, I was out for nothing but blood from whoever. Kin or not.

My shower in the master bedroom turned off, and that pulled me from my thoughts.

"Hey, daddy. How did you sleep?" Bonnie said, stepping out of the bathroom. I brought her back to my place last night after that dance she gave me. I couldn't leave her little ass there, and I damn sure wasn't about to come home wondering what that pussy felt like. Bonnie and I hadn't seen each other in a minute since I had her setup in Dallas at my homeboy, Tony's, spot.

"I slept a'ight. You gon' make some breakfast, or you got somewhere to be?" I asked.

I know this may have looked bad because my son did just die last night, but I made my best moves on a full stomach. I wasn't a dumb nigga, so I was just observing the scenes, waiting for the right time to act—for right now anyway.

Bonnie was a young, lil' chick I had been fucking with on the low. I moved her out to Dallas because I wanted her to get her shit together. I knew that if Nicki and Henn were tied to Fab and Cash, they had nothing good going for themselves, and Bonnie was so much better than that. She was young, but she had her head on her shoulders. I was forty-one, and Bonnie's little fine ass was twenty-five. She was the youngest of Henn and Nicki, so I really couldn't understand why she was fucking with them. She swore up and down Henn was her best friend, but in my opinion, ain't no best friend going to hold you back from being the best you can be.

When I first met Bonnie, she was going to school to do hair, but little did she know, I was in the process of buying her, her own shop so she could be legit. None of that kitchen shit she had been doing. Henn and Nicki knew Bonnie was good at what she did, but they never pushed her to finish school. Not saying they were her parents, but if the old ass, dusty, busted-down ass bitches were going to call themselves hanging out with her, they could've kept her on her shit. No questions asked. That's why when I started fucking with her heavy, I bossed her up.

"Babe, you know I don't have anywhere else to be. I already started cooking, and what are you thinking about that has you guided off. Do you see what I have on?" Bonnie said, placing her weight on one leg and making her ass shake. That was the good thing about fucking with a stripper. They knew how to please a nigga.

"Sorry, bae. I'm just thinking about the shit with my son and then you, man. Why you still hanging with them dirty ass hoes?" I walked over to her and grabbed a handful of her bare ass in my hands.

"What you mean, G? You know those are my bitches. Come on. We've been through this." Bonnie did a little pout with her face.

"You know that soft shit doesn't work on me. You know why I don't like you hanging with them. Them bitches ain't no good for you, cupcake, and you know that."

I licked my lips at how sexy she was. I swear to God, Bonnie brought something out of me that my last three wives never could. She challenged me, she wasn't easily satisfied, and she was smart, beautiful, and a beast in the sheets. I'm just happy I lucked up. I keep it on the low that I'm fucking with her because I don't want everybody thinking they knew what was going on between us, and I didn't want anybody feeling like they could judge. I'm glad Bonnie was cool with that. My last wife, Marquez's mom, would've never had that.

Mona, Marquez's mother, left me when Marquez turned thirteen. I woke up one morning, and she was just gone. That shit hurt my heart so bad because I really loved her. Our relationships had its ups and downs, but I guess she just found somebody better and more her paygrade. Mona was a doctor at the hospital, and at the time she and

I were together, I had just got laid off from my job. The last three years of our relationship had been nothing but argument and argument, and I really just wanted things to work for us. I would've given that woman the world on a silver platter, but her mind was already set on being with someone better than me.

One day, I was picking Marquez up from football practice, and I saw his mom out with another man. I didn't know who the nigga was, and I didn't care to, but they looked like they were fucking by the way she was giggling and shit. The same way she used to giggle with me. So ever since then, I told Marquez his mom died in a house fire, and that's how I was going to keep it. Hell, she wasn't going to try to reach out to him anyway. That's just how lousy she was.

"Just for the weekend, papa, relax. I know you're going through about what happened to Marquez last night, and honestly, I wasn't planning on leaving. If you want me to stay here with you, babe, you know I will. I don't want you going through this alone." Bonnie came and sat on my lap at the kitchen table, softly kissing my neck.

"You don't gotta worry your pretty, little head about that, mama. I've already called my boy up there, and he know you won't be back for a few weeks, but it's good because I'll keep you plenty busy." I pulled my dick out and placed it in her hand. I was a straight-up nigga, and Bonnie knew exactly what I want her to do. She pulled her panties to the side and straddled across my lap, sliding her tight, little kitty down my shaft. I grunted in satisfaction. Her shit felt just how it did last night, like I hadn't been in that shit at all.

"Fuck, G. I'm about to cum already," Bonnie moaned in my ear.

"What's stopping you, baby? You know I always let you go first." I switched positions on her ass and had her bent over the dishwasher while I dug her guts out from behind. Each stroke, Bonnie got louder and louder. It was like when I was in that pussy, I had no problems in the world. She clenched her lips around my dick. "B, you tryna have my kid? Fuck." That was a little trick that she did often, and that's why she had me wrapped around her little finger. I wasn't gon' ever stop fucking with shorty as long as she played her cards right.

"I knew you was gon' do that. You must want me to be yo' wife because you put a baby in me, you gon' have to marry me, nigga." Bonnie got herself together and went over to the stove to finish cooking breakfast.

"Shit, in due time, lil' momma. Due time." I sat there and finished the breakfast she had prepared. Bonnie's little ass could make a mean ass omelet. She knew exactly how to get right to a nigga's heart though his gut. I sat there for a moment scrolling through my notifications. I was surprised Mona hadn't called me yet. Her damn only son's death was all over the damn TV.

"Babe, what's your plans today? Nicki and Henn wanted to go get lunch, and I was going to go with them. I know you don't like me being with them, so I'll be home as soon as we leave there." Bonnie pulled me from my thoughts.

"Yeah, a'ight, and if you ain't home by the time I get back, I'm coming to find your ass. Them bitches be having you on dummy missions, and they're way older than you. They should be on some classy shit." I placed my phone back facedown.

"I know, baby. I know, but Henn is my best friend, and she needs me right now. Her and Cash got into it, and she sounds more hurt than ever. Usually, I can call her out on her bullshit, but this don't sound like the Henn I know," Bonnie admitted. She didn't even know, but she really just gave me an earful. If Cash was out here in Henn's face, I know Nicki wasn't too far behind stirring some shit up.

"What you mean? They broke up or something?" I questioned. This was my chance to hit these little niggas where it hurt. They wanted to play a grown-man game. I had one for their asses. That little, pretty bitch Fab was fucking with, I was going to fuck her little foreign ass and show that nigga what hurt was.

"Yeah, basically. I mean, she said he said some cruel ass shit to her, and she didn't want to say it over the phone, but of course, he making it official again with Cambria, and Fab with that new chick."

"Shorty from the party right? Lil' foreign chick? I figured they had something the way he was talking to her all close up on her."

"Yeah, well, that's what happened, so what's your plans?" Bonnie fingered with her food for a bit.

"I'ma just chill out today, ma. Have fun with ya girls." I smiled mischievously.

Pow! Pow! Pow!

The glass in my living room shattered, and I pushed Bonnie's barely-clothed body to the ground. As Bonnie screamed at the top of her lungs, I was feeling my pockets for my piece, and I didn't have it on me. We lay there on the cold kitchen floor for a moment until the gunshots ceased. I was mad that somebody had just caught me lacking in my own shit. I suggested we lay there for at least ten more minutes after the shots were fired to make sure they were gone. I already knew who was playing games, and it was my baby brother, Bruce. If he really wanted to make a move, he would've killed me. He had every opportunity to, but he didn't want to. He called himself sending a warning.

"Babe, does somebody have money on your head? What's going on, baby? You can talk to me, G. You know that." Bonnie kissed me on my lips.

I stood in place thinking of my next move. I couldn't be sitting here bullshitting when my brother had it out for me. I really wasn't trying to make any sudden moves until after the funeral of my son, because the fingers would point directly to me, and I would either get killed in the streets or in the pen. I couldn't have that. I needed things to die down a little bit before I did anything.

"Nah. I don't know who that could be. You know I stay to myself. I don't be in no bullshit. Call my window man. Tell him come fix this shit, and you go chill with your girls. I'ma go handle some shit, and then we are hitting the road." I revealed we were going to Dallas for a little bit to my Tony's spot. Anytime I would come up there to see Bonnie, I would link up with him. I just recently moved to Atlanta a year ago. I was fucking with Marquez's mom on the road from my trips back and forth.

"Alright, babe. I'll call you when we're done, and you can just come get me from Nicki's spot."

"Cool." We both hopped in the shower, got dressed, and went on about our day like nothing had happened. That's why I fucked with Bonnie. She was a young rider. She rolled with the punches of any circumstance. Little Bruce just started a big war for himself.

I hopped in my Cadillac and headed to the other side of town. I couldn't be seen on this side, because I wasn't trying to die before I let my brother know he could never equate to me. My brother thought he couldn't be touched, but that's where he went wrong. Ever since Pops died, he thought he was almighty. Even growing up, the nigga would act like he was older than me. Every time we would play "cops and robbers", he would always want me to be the cop like I was too square to be a robber. That shit used to piss me off. I knew I couldn't complain to my momma, because I would look like a little bitch.

Damn, I missed my momma, man. She died a few years

back. That's when the real war started between me and Bruce because the same year my mom died, my dad died, and that's when he told us how he felt and why he thought it was a good reason to give Bruce the streets instead of me.

I finally pulled up to the bar and grill across town where I went inside and ordered a burger and a beer. I grabbed something light because this wasn't the time to eat. This was the time to think and get my ducks in a row. Starting tonight, I was going to pick Bonnie up from Nicki's. We were going to plan my son's funeral. Second, I was going to fuck Fab's girl, and last, but not least, own the streets like I was supposed to from the beginning while living with my brother's murder over my head. I smiled at the thought of that. Uncle Gutta wasn't the one to be fucked with. Once you crossed the line with me, you needed to stay there.

9

Bonnie

"A'ight, baby. Be easy. Don't do nothing stupid, and we can meet back at the crib. I love you," Gutta said.

I had Henn and Nicki thinking I was staying at a hotel because I didn't want them to know I was dating Gutta. Everybody's business wasn't nobody's business, and I was going to keep it that way. Gutta and I were so much happier that nobody knew about us, except Henn and Nicki, and that was because they figured it out themselves, but no one else knew. I made them swear not to tell a soul. Shit, being low key made the sex ten times better.

"I love you too, babe, be safe, and I won't be long," I said, kissing his lips as I played with his beard. Something about a man having hair on his face was such a turn on to me.

I loved my relationship with Gutta so much. I had

never been with an older man before, but we hit it off immediately. He was so intelligent, and he was highly slept on. I knew him and his younger brother didn't get along from the stories he used to tell me. But to have his son killed and his house shot up was another type of beef that I felt like I was unaware of. I wished I could get to the bottom of shit how Henn, Nicki, and I would, but I didn't want Gutta to think I was back to our old ways.

I saw how Gutta tried to hide the pain of his son's death, but he wasn't doing a very good job, because I knew him probably better than he knew himself. When Gutta and I first met, it was like an immediate spark. From his smile down to the way he held me, everything was so different with him than it was with other men I've danced for before. Gutta was the type to have his own wife and kids at home, not to be in the strip club, and I think that's what attracted me to him.

Most niggas just wanted to fuck, and that was it. I was so tired of being everybody's one-night stand. I felt like I had the potential to be a wife. That's why I was so submissive to him. He was everything I dreamed for in a man, and seeing him trying to hide his hurt made me want to fuck somebody up. When Gutta told me we were going back to Dallas until he thought shit through, I knew he really had something big he was plotting on, and I wanted him to know that I was down for whatever.

He was my only family, and I was his. My mom and dad both started abusing drugs when I was a little girl. I was only fifteen years old. I was thankful that we still had somewhere to lay our heads, and the only reason we still had that was because my mom paid it off within her first year of being a doctor. My mom was a doctor, and my dad used to be a corporate manager at a bank. I know you're probably wondering how they got from those successful lifestyles to rock bottom, literally.

It all started when my dad got laid off from his job when I first turned fourteen. My mom prescribed him some medicine for depression and anxiety, thinking it would help him cope. But they both started using them together. Really, I don't even know at which point in my mom's life she became so addicted to prescribed medications, but Xanax was her favorite candy.

In the beginning, they were just doing it together occasionally. They would always promise me they would stop. I came home with my friend Julia one day and caught them drugged up in their bedroom. I remember I cried myself to sleep that night. I just wanted things to be back to how they were.

My phone started vibrating as I jumped into my car and headed to the nearest diner to eat with Nicki and Henn.

"Hello? Bonnie, baby, what's up?" Tony's voice blared through the phone. I was so tired of him calling me, but I knew if I didn't answer this time, he was going to continue to.

"What do you want, Tony? I told you to leave me

alone." I rolled my eyes as I waited for him to say some bullshit. He had been trying to get at me since Gutta first introduced us, but I told him that could never happen. Ever. He was lucky I didn't tell Gutta that he was making me feel uncomfortable. It would've be over for his ass then.

"Chill, Bonnie, boo. I can't call you and check up on you? You know we had something special with that kiss. Why are you fronting?" Tony was so annoying. It wasn't a damn kiss. He forced himself on me, and that's as far as he got because I kicked him in his nuts.

"Bye before I tell Gutta," I said before disconnecting the call. I don't know why I was hiding that from Gutta, but I just knew the time wasn't right, right now. I was going to tell him last night, but then all of that shit happened with his son. I just hoped that he wouldn't say anything before I got the chance to. I felt the chills run down my spine at just the thought of Tony touching me the way he did. You know what? I was going to tell Gutta tonight. Maybe he would want to kill him.

When I arrived at the diner, Nicki and Henn were already there. Henn looked like she had been crying for days straight. I had never seen my friend down so bad, but maybe she was finally starting to see Cash for who he really was. In my opinion, it was no way I'm playing side bitch to a nigga that treats me like shit. He at least got to wine and dine me. Henn was just being dumb staying wrapped up with him, and she knew it, I knew it—hell, everybody knew it.

"Henn, baby, are you alright? We're going to pull through this, man. Please don't let that trash ass nigga get the best of you," I said, trying to comfort her, but I wanted so badly to say, "bitch, I told you so!" She never listened, and then when shit like this here happened, she was crying, looking all ugly and shit.

"I'm really trying not to let it get to me that much, but I love Cash so much, man, and I know he feels the same, but after what he said, it really has me second guessing everything." Henn began to start with the water works again.

"Bitch, tell her, or I will." Nicki intervened. I could tell she was mad as hell. Nicki was like Henn's protector even though she was younger than Henn. I didn't know why Henn acted so naïve, but for her age, she should've been way past this "crying over niggas" stage. I mean, she was my best friend, and I loved her to death, but maybe Gutta was right; I was outgrowing them.

"I am, Nicki. Shut up! You always want to tell somebody else's story. Tell her what Fab did to your stupid ass." Henn sounded defensive as hell, and I just sat there looking from Nicki to Henn, waiting on who was going to speak first.

"I had an abortion a few weeks ago. I was calling Cash while he was with Bria one night. I mean, I didn't know they were together, but that shouldn't matter. I'm the mother of his kids. Anyway, when I brought it up to him how much I sacrificed, all he had to say was, 'you brought that on yourself, and you knew I was fucking with Bria heavy. Didn't nobody tell you to get pregnant in the first place. I pretended to care about them abortions, but I didn't. I already knew you wasn't the one for me, just someone I could fuck with while Bria was in one of her moods.' I can't believe he said that shit. Do you know how bad that hurt? I thought he cared for me." Henn's tears were now flowing heavier than ever. I grabbed her hand across from the table. I felt for her.

"Whoa, wait. He said all of that? You had a damn abortion a few weeks ago and didn't tell me?" I asked question after question. I was curious as to why she was keeping shit from me.

"I didn't want to tell anybody because I was embarrassed. Like this is my fourth one... like really," Henn cried.

I felt so bad for my friend because she really didn't deserve that. Henn deserved someone who gave a fuck about her, and I couldn't stress that enough. I don't know how many times I had to tell her, but it was getting old. I really needed her to catch a grip on life.

"OK, listen, I'll never ever judge you, Henn, and I want you to get that out of your head, but I will tell you if you don't boss up on this nigga and move on with your life, I don't know if I can be your friend anymore," I replied bluntly. It was no way for me to try to sugarcoat anything. I wasn't about to keep sitting around watching her move backward with this nigga. They were getting nowhere, and she was in a way worse situation than she was when she started messing with him. I was sick of it.

"So you would really cut me off because of who I love?" Henn looked up with a screwed-u[face. I don't know why her ass was looking like that as if I hadn't told her all of this before.

"Yes, you are exactly right. I'm tired of seeing you hurt, damn! What the fuck? You should want more for yourself as a woman," I mentioned, now taking a sip of my lemonade that the waiter had brought.

"She's right though, Henn. That's not love. That nigga keep doing you dirty constantly. That's not love, baby girl. He knows your situation, but not once has he offered you to come stay with him or anything. He's just not for you, and it's that simple." Nicki agreed.

It was crazy that Nicki and I were on the same page because when Henn first introduced us, we didn't get along at all, and I don't know if it was because we were around the same age or she was jealous that it was a new bitch in the crew, but that bitch couldn't stand me, and I couldn't stand her. We actually just grew on each other. Nicki was a good person, but she was still whipped on her baby daddy, but that was another story for another time.

"Crazy part about this whole conversation is y'all said y'all would never judge me, and here y'all are judging me. You know what? I'm out. I'm done here, and don't call me. I'm turning my phone off," Henn said, sliding out of the booth.

"Wait!" I called to Henn.

"Henn, come back!" Nicki pleaded. Henn threw up her

middle finger and exited the diner, soon waving down a cab. I wasn't worried. She wouldn't go far, and she would be back. I just hated she wasted my time coming here if she wasn't going to be an adult and hear our side.

"It's crazy that we are younger than her, and she is acting like that, Nicki. For real." I rolled my eyes and began eating my food. When I said I wasn't worried about it, I really wasn't. Henn didn't have anywhere to go, so I knew she would be back at Nicki's later.

"Girl, you know her dramatic ass always have to cause a scene. It's all good though. She'll be back. What you up to today?" Nicki asked.

"Nothing really. I'm probably going to go back to Dallas early. It isn't anything here for me anyway." I shrugged my shoulders briefly.

"I wish I could come to Dallas, man. I would love to make that money you make, but I don't have anybody to keep Aubrey, especially with her ain't-shit ass daddy." Nicki was about to start up on her baby daddy, and I could already tell where this conversation was going.

"Hello, yeah. I'm coming right now. Send me the address." I put my phone to my ear, pretending to be on a phone call, knowing damn well nobody was on the other line. I just needed a quick escape from Nicki and her bull-shit. She was my friend and all, but I had shit going on too, and I needed to make sure my man was straight because this is when he needed me the most.

"You aren't about to go, are you?" Nicki questioned.

"Girl, yes. I have to. I'm so sorry. Here, I'll pay. Text me when you get home and let me know if Henn is there." I placed a fifty-dollar bill on the table.

"Oh, OK, girl. I will. See you soon. Safe travels," Nicki said as if I had just let her down. I really didn't care how she felt. I was low-key pissed off about how Henn reacted to me being honest to her, and I wasn't in the mood to hear about anybody else's bullshit.

GUTTA and I had finally landed in Dallas, and I was more nervous now than I was before to tell him about Tony. I didn't know why, but I guess it was because I didn't want Gutta to think I wanted him to kiss me, because it was far from that. When we arrived at Tony's house, I was hoping that he wasn't there, because that would've made things even more awkward. As we walked up his driveway, I could feel my anxiety worsening because his car was in the yard, and I knew that meant he was home.

"Babe, wait, I need to tell you something before you go in here, and this nigga be all buddy-buddy in your face." I finally spoke up, but I could tell that my voice was shaking.

"What's up, B? What's wrong, baby?" Gutta grabbed my chin and looked me in my eyes.

"Tony tried to fuck me. He pushed himself on me and kissed me. I kicked him in his nuts when he tried to pull my pants down. I wanted to tell you, Gutta, but I didn't want you to think I wanted that man, because that is not the case. I was going to tell you last night, but that shit happened with Marquez, and then the bullets flying through your house. It was just a lot going on. Please don't be mad at me." I looked up in Gutta's eyes, and I couldn't read his expression at all.

He didn't say a thing as he grabbed my hand, and we continued to walk to the door. I didn't question him. I just followed behind him. I watched as he pulled his gun from his back pocket. I still didn't say a word as we headed to the door. Gutta knocked a few times, and Tony finally opened it.

"Hey, bro. What's good? Bonnie, what's up?" Tony said, going in for a dap from Gutta.

"Nah, don't fake the funk, my nigga. You tried to fuck my shorty?" Gutta inquired.

"Chill. You know it's brothers before these hoes. She wanted that shi—"

Gutta sent two bullets through his head. I watched as Tony's body fell limp, and he immediately started to bleed out.

"Bonnie, don't ever keep shit from me again. Go pack all your shit. We don't need a trace of either of us here. We are going to take a ride. I'll clean this up." Gutta kissed my forehead, and I stepped over Tony's body and headed upstairs to pack my stuff like he said.

Strangely, I didn't feel any type of way about Gutta killing Tony. I wasn't scared or anything. When I came back downstairs, Gutta had Tony sitting on the couch with the gun in his hand and a letter he had written as if it was a suicide note. I stood there smiling because this shit just made Gutta so much sexier to me. He really killed a nigga for me, and that shit right there spoke volumes to me. Bitches was out here begging they niggas to even say something to a nigga, and mine just killed a motherfucker without warning. I could so suck his dick right now.

"A'ight. Let's go, baby," Gutta said, and we headed straight to the car with my bags. We found a nice suite about thirty minutes away, and we stayed there. The room was so nice. I didn't think I had ever been in something so nice before. I was so thankful for Gutta because he really introduced me to real something these other niggas couldn't. We spent an entire week just enjoying each other's company and planning for Marquez's funeral. I knew this was going to be the hardest time for Gutta, and I didn't want to be anywhere else but next to him.

10

Nicki

I had been calling Bonnie for three days straight, and not once had she answered the phone. I was beyond worried about Henn. She hadn't been home since the night at the diner. What I couldn't understand was why did she wasn't answering the phone. The way Bonnie left the diner the other day, I was really feeling some type of way, but I didn't speak on it because she wasn't really my friend; she was Henn's.

Bonnie and I never usually seen eye to eye, but at this very moment, I needed her more than ever because my cousin was missing. I know Henn was dramatic. I mean, she had always been that way since we were growing up, but this wasn't like her to go missing. I didn't want to call the police, because I didn't want them involved if it wasn't that serious.

Today was the day of Marquez's funeral, and I already knew for a fact Bonnie was going to be there because I mean, of course, her and Gutta had something going on. I was so thankful that my grandmother was going to watch Aubrey because I didn't want her around the bullshit that was going to pop off at the funeral.

I wasn't sure if anything was going to happen, but for some reason, I had a gut feeling it was. It felt so weird pulling up at the church without Henn, but a little part of me was praying that she would be sitting somewhere in the audience when I got there. When I walked in the church ,the first person I laid my eyes on was Fab, and he was with that bitch I had seen him with before.

He was real bold bringing this bitch to his cousin's funeral, that he fucking killed, knowing that I was going to be there. I was going to try my best to stay on my best behavior because this wasn't the time for that. I found me a seat at the back of the church and watched as everyone walked up to view the body, and they began to fill seats.

I didn't even expect for the funeral to be this packed, but hey, I guess that's how it goes when you're a hood nigga. I made sure to observe the crowd because I was sure I was going to see Bonnie. When I finally seen her walk in with Gutta, I could tell that she had been crying. I rolled my eyes. She had time to grieve but not to answer the phone when she was the one that told me to call anyway?

Oddly, she didn't sit next to Gutta. I was sitting back here with my bitter ass, peeping out the whole scene. I was nosy, so it wasn't hard. I couldn't help but to keep my focus on Cambria, Fab, Cash, and his new bitch that wasn't even worth mentioning her name. I turned my attention back to the pastor as he went on about how this wasn't something we needed to be depressed about; this was a celebration of life. I wasn't really a church person, so I shoved my head-phones in my ears and just vibed to music until I seen everyone getting up to leave.

Before the service was over, Gutta mentioned that he was having a cookout at his mansion for his son. I didn't need an invite. I was pulling up anyway because I had some bones to pick with Bonnie.

"Please, don't come to my house on any bullshit, because I'm bound to kill me a motherfucker today." Gutta dropped the microphone on the podium as if he just rapped the best bars ever produced.

"Boy, bye," I mumbled. I was siding with Henn so much when she said Gutta moved Bonnie away so she couldn't be near us that I truly believed that. What kind of nigga would want his girl to not have friends? I rolled my eyes at the thought of his pit-bull-looking ass. I jumped in my car and headed to Gutta's mansion. I was not only ready to talk to Bonnie, but Fab's little girlfriend too.

I usually would have Henn here encouraging me, but I guess I was going to have to show my ass by myself. But I was completely fine with that because I felt like I was the most hype out of the group any damn way. These bitches were ready to settle down and shit. Ol' "want to be a wife head" asses. I pulled my 2007 black Honda on the side of Gutta's house and waited for everybody to arrive. I was the first to get there, but that was because I wanted to get the best parking, and I needed to get my eyes on Fab.

I pulled my phone out and tried to call Henn one more time, but she didn't answer, as expected. I thought I had a glimpse of her at the funeral, but I could've been tripping. I didn't get any sleep last night, so I had taken a Xanax at five in the morning to help me sleep, but that one didn't work, so I took another one, and it had me floating. I was up. Good thing I didn't have bags under my eyes, because I couldn't go out like that. I couldn't have bags under my eyes going to this funeral especially. I needed to show Fab what his dumb ass was missing out on. He always wanted to play tit for tat, but he had the right one because I was winning this battle.

I jumped out of my car, throwing my phone in my pocket and slamming the door as I saw Fab walk across the lawn. I couldn't wait to get my hands around his scrawny, lying ass neck. I sped across the lawn, almost to my destination.

"Hey, Nicki. I didn't know you were coming to the funeral. Where is Henn?" Bonnie asked, pulling my attention away from Fab.

"Bitch, I was in the middle of something." I huffed.

"Middle of what?" Bonnie's eyebrows pulled together as if she was confused. I sucked my teeth.

"Nothing, girl. Where have you been? I've been calling

your ass, and it sure hasn't been because I missed you. Henn is missing. She hasn't been home since the diner, and you know this isn't like her." I began engaging in the conversation more now that it was about my cousin. I really did miss her and was worried.

"Wait, what? You didn't call me." Bonnie pulled her phone out showing me her call log where there were no missing calls.

"Bitch, bye. You probably deleted it." I went to my contacts and pulled the number up I had for her and showed her.

"Girl, that's not my fucking number, that's why," Bonnie said. I huffed. That's why she wasn't answering. I was blowing her phone up—well, what I thought was her phone—and it wasn't even the right number.

"Well, anyway, we need to find her," I replied.

"Duh, but not tonight because I owe Gutta my undivided attention. Come on. Let's go inside," Bonnie said as she led the way back to her house.

This nigga didn't even sit with you at the funeral, but you need to show him your undivided attention? This bitch was beyond me. I didn't say anything though, because she would've sworn I was trying to be funny or jealous, and I didn't have time to whoop her ass at her boyfriend's shit. I just needed to curse Fab out first, make a little scene, and then I was leaving, with or without Bonnie.

. . .

JOSIE "JO"

I felt so out of place being at Gutta's mansion. I understood that he didn't want any drama, but I could just tell the vibe was off. I ran my fingers through my hair and followed behind Fab while Cambria and Cash followed behind me. The music blared loud through the large home, and people were standing around drinking and dancing like it was an actual party. Stepping into the front house, I could see the back of the house, and he had a large patio and swimming pool.

Naked bitches were everywhere. It was disgusting if you asked me. I mean, people grieved differently. I assumed I couldn't talk because I did link up with Fab my first night in Atlanta. Honestly, I was glad that I did. Fab was such a gentleman. He was hardcore on the outside and soft on the inside. I couldn't stop thinking about how he held me and opened up to me the night we stayed in the suite after the party.

When we left the church and arrived at Gutta's house, Fab grabbed his gun from his glove compartment and told me to stay close and let him know if anybody was bothering me. I just felt like he was acting a bit overprotective. I don't know, Maybe that was just him.

Best, let's go get some punch, Bria mouthed to me.

"Lead the way," I replied.

"Come on, y'all. I'm coming." Fab said.

"No need. We aren't babies. We'll be fine." Bria swatted

him off as she led the way to the bowl. Grabbing my cup from her, I took a sip.

"Drink another, and pour you another shot, boo," Bria said.

"Whoo, shit!" I said, pulling the cup away from my lips.

"It's spiked! Have fun," Bria said, dancing through the crowd. I followed behind her until I felt someone yank me into a room.

"Don't scream, or I'll blow your fucking brains out. Plus, nobody can hear you over this loud ass music." Gutta's hot breath made the food I had earlier turn in my stomach.

"You so damn pretty. I'd been eyeing your ass since I saw you at my birthday bash. What yo' lil' foreign ass doing all the way out here?" Gutta licked his lips and then pulled me in for a hard kiss.

"Get off me! What the fuck is wrong with you?" I slapped him hard in the face.

"That's exactly what I wanted you to do. You didn't know I liked it rough, baby girl?" Gutta pushed me down on the bed and yanked my pants down while unbuckling his as the same time.

"Please, no! Stop!" I cried, trying to fight him off of me, but the more I fought, it felt like the stronger he got. I felt my body become limp and weak as I lay there crying. Gutta pounded himself in and out of me, dripping sweat on my face, and I tried to squirm away. It didn't take him long as he took advantage of my body, and I felt like I was being stripped of everything all over again, just like I was in Brazil.

"This is for your bitch ass boyfriend killing my son. Now, now, baby, this dick is the least of your worries. This belongs to Bonnie. If you tell anyone what happened, I'll kill Fab. Just how I took away your pride, I can take away his breath in the blink of an eye. You don't know this family," Gutta said, getting himself together as he got dressed and exited the room.

Why did Cambria leave me? Why would she do that, and she knows we're at this party together? I should've just stayed with Fab. I got myself together and threw some water on my face. I stood there for at least three more minutes crying. I washed my face again and decided I was going to tell Fab and curse Bria the fuck out after Fab handled his ass. I was done running from my problems. If Gutta wanted to include me in their shit, I was now included. Let the games begin, bitch.

When I stepped out the bathroom, it was like no one that was standing there had noticed what was going on or what would just happened. I pulled a weak smile on my face and headed to the bowl Bria and I were at to get another drink. When I finally found Fab, some bitch was in his face, which completely took my attention off of what I really had going on. When I approached, I stood back to see what was being said.

"So you really doing me like this? Bringing this bitch around your family? The same family that you brought me around!" the woman yelled, pointing in his face. I could look by his expression that he was getting angrier by the minute. I stepped to get a better view of the girl, and it was the same chick that was with that girl that Bria knocked out in the club, and she was staring. Who the hell was she?

"Get the fuck out of my face, Nicki. We've already been through this, and I'm not about to keep going through it with you, man. Just let me live my damn life." Fab caught eyes with me.

"Bitch, back the fuck up off my nigga." I felt a side of me that I didn't even know I had in me, but whatever. I was tired of motherfuckers trying to walk all over me.

"No, bitch! You back the fuck up! You don't even know me! Did this motherfucker even tell you he had a baby?" Nicki turned her attention from me to him. I was shocked as hell, but I wasn't going to let that bitch know anything. I wasn't going to start us and Fab off like that. A big crowd had now gathered around us.

"He sure did. Now what? I supposed to have a problem with that or what? Like what did you expect? For me to stop fucking with him? You seem real bothered right now, babe. You're beautiful. Go get your own man." Somebody from the crowd started laughing at my remark, and then it was like one person after the other. I could see the anger and embarrassment in her face.

"Yeah, so step. I told you all of this could've been avoided," Fab said.

"You right it could have." Hennessy stood from afar while holding a gun in her hand.

"Henn, oh my God! Where have you been? I've missed you," Nicki said, trying to approach her cousin.

"Leave me the fuck alone with your judgmental ass. You swear you gave a fuck, but you here at this party worried about some nigga." Henn now stood in the middle of the party with her gun facing Nicki. I watched as everyone stood there and watched everything unfold.

"Henn, you know I love you. It was Bonnie's idea to wait until after the party." Nicki searched the room with her eyes trying to find someone.

"That doesn't even matter. I didn't come here for all of that. My bone is to pick with Cash and his little girlfriend," Hennessy said.

"You don't have shit to say to my man," Bria said, now coming out the cut. Before, I didn't see here.

"Baby, he's only yours because we're done. Cash, I can't believe you left me for this bitch. I can't believe you made me get numerous abortions because you didn't want to have children because you weren't ready. What about me and what I want?"

"Wait... Cash, so you mean to tell me you got this tired-pussy ass hoe pregnant not once, but multiple times?" Bria snapped on Cash. As usual, he just stood there like he had no care in the world. Hennessy having a gun didn't even faze him.

"Bria, baby girl, don't listen to this bitch. She's delusional." Cash put his cup to his lips.

"Cash, you're a fucking liar, and you know I was pregnant with your babies. It's like that though? You're hiding the fact that you got me pregnant. Not that I didn't mind at the time, because I thought we were going to be together, but you've played me for the last time." Hennessy pulled the gun up higher and aimed it at Cambria. "If I can't have you, she sure as hell won't!" Before Fab could pull his gun, she pulled the trigger. Cash immediately jumped in front of Bria, and the crowd that was there before was now gone.

The only people that stood in the room were Fab, Bria, Cash, Bonnie, Nicki, Gutta, and me. Where Nicki and Gutta came from, I didn't know, but the sight of him disgusted me so much. At that moment, I wished I had a gun because I would've splattered his brains all over his living room wall. Henn fired two bullets hitting both Cambria and Cash.

Fab pulled his gun and fired two shots at Henn, hitting her once in the leg and then the arm, causing her to drop the gun to the floor. Bria and Cash both fell to the ground as blood rushed from their wounds.

"Bitch, what did you do?" I screamed, rushing toward Henn. I didn't know what had overcome me, but I was about to beat the living shit out of her, bleeding out or not. I kicked her in the stomach first and climbed on top of her while I punched her in the face continuously. I completely blacked out. I came back to reality when I felt someone pull me off her. To my surprise, it was Fab. I had blood all over my white dress, and she lay there unconscious.

"You for real? Like you're dead serious right now, Fab!" Nicki called as Fab led me out the house before the police came in and seen me letting it loose on her ass.

"Thank you, Fab. But where is Bria?" I searched through the crowd and then switched my eyes to the EMS trucks that were parked out front.

"Baby, don't thank me. I didn't even know yo' ass had that in you. I was almost scared to pull you off. But you're riding with me to get a change of clothes, and we're heading to the hospital." Fab grabbed my hand and pulled me to his car, trying not to be seen by the police. That's the last thing we needed.

I WAS SO happy to be at the hospital. I mean, we were waiting to hear back about Bria and Cash, but I felt a sense of relief because I took all my anger out on the bitch who shot Bria. On the other hand, I was a bit overwhelmed because of all the shit that happened between Gutta and myself. We hadn't seen him at the hospital, and I was thankful for that. I wanted to tell Fab so bad about what happened, but I knew this wasn't the time.

After waiting for hours and hours, the doctors finally came out. "Cambria Wilson's family?" The doctor approached us in the tiny corner we were sitting in.

"Yes, we're right here. Fabio's her older brother." Fab held his hand out to shake the doctors.

"Jo' her best friend," I added.

"Nice to meet you guys. I'm Doctor Taylor. I want you guys to know that we were able to get most of the bullet out—"

"Most of it out? What do you mean? What about the rest of it? Is she alright?" Fab cut the doctor off in mid-sentence.

"This happens all the time. The first bullet went through her and ricocheted into Cash. The second bullet was in her leg. It seemed like the bullet that went through and through caused the most damage. She is in stable condition, luckily, but she's in a coma," Dr. Taylor said.

"Coma? Wait... huh? Are you sure?" I questioned this wasn't supposed to happen like this. I felt the tears stinging at my eyes.

"How long is she supposed to be in a coma, Doc?" Fab replied.

"As of right now, we aren't able to tell. It could be anywhere from a few weeks to months. What she really needs right now is for the both of you to be strong for her. If you would like, you can go in and see her," Dr. Taylor mentioned.

I stood there letting the tears flow because what was I going to do now? I wished bitches weren't so bitter and hateful. This could've all been avoided. "Wait, what about Cash Jones?" I asked.

"Mr. Jones is still in surgery. We had to resuscitate him twice, but things are looking alright for him. The bad thing about his surgery is we won't be able to know the outcome until he actually wakes up. Once he is out of surgery, I'll keep you guys informed so you can visit him as well. You guys stay strong. This shall pass," Dr. Taylor assured us before he walked away.

This was so much to take in. When we walked into Bria's room, she didn't even look like herself. She looked so frail with that large breathing tube down her throat. I just didn't imagine ever seeing my best friend on a ventilator. I immediately ran to her bedside. I felt so bad for her situation. When I turned to look at Fab, he had tears in her eyes.

"Why didn't I shoot sooner, man? Why didn't I see this shit coming?" Fab continued to blame himself while I grabbed him and held on to him.

"Stop blaming yourself, Fab. There was nothing that either of us could've done. Things were going to happen how they wanted to. We had no control over the situation, nor could we stop that. We just have to be strong for her now. That's our only option. That's the only thing we can do," I cried.

"You're right. I need to tighten up and make a few phone calls. I don't know if my dad and mom have heard, but I need to call them. Do you mind sitting up here for a minute while I step out and make some calls?" Fab asked.

"It's fine. I understand. I need to be with her right now

anyway." I turned my attention back to Bria. I just wanted my friend back. I needed her so bad right now, and to think I was mad at her because of the shit that happened with Gutta, but I couldn't even be mad anymore, even if I wanted to. I couldn't wait for my best friend to wake up. I needed her just as bad as she needed me.

11

Cambria "Bria"

I jumped out of the shower, and I heard my phone ringing. I just wanted to get away from this crazy ass city. My brother killed our blood cousin almost a full week ago, and my dad had something do with it, but nobody was telling me anything. I just wanted all of this shit to end. A vacation was more than needed right now. I looked at my screen and seen it was Fab calling.

"What's up, killa?" I emphasized.

"Chill. Don't call me that, sis. I was just calling to see if you wanted to go board a flight to Cancun. I was thinking we all need a vacation, especially after last night," Fab said. It was like he was taking the thoughts right out of my head and bringing them to reality. Getting out of Atlanta was exactly what I needed.

"Hell yes! I would love to. How did you know? Shit, I know Jo' would be down because she needs to see some new shit. She's

only been here for a few weeks and seen more than her ass can handle. Shit, me too!"

"Did you say vacation?" Jo' asked.

"Girl, yes. Paid in full by Fab. We're leaving tomorrow. Cancun bitch!" I yelled.

"A'ight. Hit me when y'all ready to be picked up tomorrow morning. I'm about to get some shit in order. Just wanted to let you know the moves," Fab said as he ended the call.

"Girl, you know last night, Cash held me all night—well, morning—while I cried, and I didn't even say two words to him. I think I want to give him another chance. I truly believe he loves me. He makes me feel it all the time when we're together." I plopped down on my bed, still in my towel.

"You know love is a beautiful thing, and if he's willing to be the best man that he can be for you, then, honey, go for it. But you have to communicate first. You can't just assume. You need to see where his head is. You know I support anything you do, but if he gets on bullshit, I'll beat his ass myself." Jo' ended the conversation and left me there in deep thought.

HERE WE ARE, the next morning, packing our last items that we felt we needed. I was so excited about going on a vacation with Jo'. This was going to be our first trip together, and I was excited. I just wanted to get my mind off things, and I knew this would be the perfect opportunity. Although, Jo' didn't know

Marquez, I felt like his death made us so much closer. We both lost a piece of our family, so shit, it was equal.

"Aye, ma, where you think you going with all them bags?" Cash stood in front of me as I was heading out the door.

"Um, why is there two cars?" I questioned because the airport where we were boarding our flight was like a hot two hours away. We wanted to get cheaper flights so we could spend more money there buying cute shit. I mean, that was my logic considering I was the one paying for the tickets. I loved to spend money, but not on airplane tickets, on sexy, new clothes.

"You are riding with me. Fab and Jo' riding together." Cash grabbed my bags and began to put them in the back seat.

I was confused as hell because this wasn't a part of the plan. I stood there with a screwed-up face because my brother really had me fucked up. I turned around, looking and Jo', and she had an ugly smile on her face. That bitch must've had something to do with this. She all for that communication shit, and I didn't know if I was ready to talk to Cash right now, especially about my feelings.

The night we got the suite together, after Fab killed Marquez, I didn't talk to him at all. I just laid in the bed and cried. He held me, but that didn't mean I was ready to talk about it. Just a sweet gesture. Cash was my baby, don't get me wrong, but I got to thinking about what Jo' said, and me and Cash really have been through a lot. I needed him to show me how he felt instead of constantly telling me.

"Oh, y'all think this shit cute? I got something for y'all, just wait." I put my shades on the top of my head and hopped in the

passenger seat. I was so dramatic. I didn't even know why I had these shades on. It was fifty-seven degrees outside.

"What's up with you, Bria?" Cash finally broke the silence thirty minutes into the drive. I wasn't going to speak to him first, and maybe I was being childish, but I don't care. It was what it was.

"What do you mean what's up with me? Is something supposed to be up? What's up with you is what I should be asking."

"If you got something you want to get off of your chest, say that shit then, Bria. Don't beat around the bush with me. You know I don't like them kiddy ass guessing games."

"You know what, Cash, actually, I do. You talk all day about how you don't fuck with Henn, and she is nothing compared to me, but yet and still, you find some way to talk to her. You find some way every time to embarrass me. Like it's ridiculous, dude! I'm all for you. I'm not out here on no bullshit. Niggas know what's up with me! But I can't say the same about you." I could feel the tears now steaming down my face.

I hadn't showed any emotion about how I really felt, but Cash was breaking me, and he acted like he didn't even notice it. I didn't want to worry about his raggedy ass, stank ass hoes popping up in our picture trying to disturb my peace, because I wasn't having it.

"Come on, ma. Don't cry, man. You know I don't like when you do all that, man, for real." Cash switched his eyes from me back to the road repeatedly.

"Well, don't make me cry, Cash." I was now sobbing, and it

was no hiding these tears. I was literally sitting in the passenger seat of this man's car blowing snot everywhere.

"Ma, listen, I love you with everything in me. Hennessy been trying to tell me that she still wanna be with me, and she might me pregnant, but I haven't even fucked her in a bop. To be honest with you, she sucked my dick the other night, and that was it. That was only because you were mad at me. I realize now that the shit mad lame. Bria, I don't like you being mad at me, and we weren't on good terms. I hate that shit. I just want to be the best man that I can be for you, man. That's why I told that bitch Henn if she bang my line again, I'm have her beat the fuck up. I'm changing my number, and all ties are cut. I don't want shorty. Only you."

"Cash, you gon' have to show me, and that's all I'm going to say on that." I wiped my tears. I was so tired of crying. I just wanted to live my best life.

"I hear that, and I'm willing, but this what you not gone do. Don't have no lame ass nigga all up in your face at the club and shit unless you want them to die," Cash said.

"Die?" I chuckled.

"Yeah, no cap. You know I'm 'bout my shit, so all I'm saying is try it again, and you better hope that nigga has life insurance," Cash said with a stern face. I knew he meant business, but if he knew me any, he knew I was good for testing his gangster.

"I hear you, Cash, but this doesn't mean we're together. It means we're taking things slow," I mentioned.

"Yeah, that's what your mouth says, but wait 'til you get on this vacation with me and see a different side of me." Cash smiled confidently.

"Whatever, nigga. Don't get out of the city and start trying to act like the world's greatest bachelor." I laughed at my comment. I always cracked myself up with my smart-ass comebacks.

"But on a serious note, when you gon' let me taste fat mama?" Cash said referring to my cat. I knew one thing usually led to another with Cash, and I wasn't trying to have sex with him, but some head did sound lovely.

"You can taste her, but please understand we are not fucking." I put my headphones in and tuned Cash out the rest of the way. We had like an hour left, and I was trying to play hard to get, even though I was excited that he wanted to eat me up. I smiled with satisfaction because that was just what I needed to keep me going. Cash had a mouth on him, and I knew his tongue would do me some justice.

"Yeah, a'ight." Cash nodded and turned the music up as he drove to the airport. I placed my headphones in my ears and let my music drown him and his music out. Cash might've got some of this wetness when we reached Cancun. It just depended on how I was feeling. I wasn't used to being in a drought of sex. This was one of the hardest things for me, but believe me when I say, it wouldn't last long. I felt like I had Cash right where I wanted him, and I was going to tease him a little bit longer just to watch him suffer a little. I closed my eyes as the music blasted through my headset, and I drifted off to sleep the rest of the ride. I was just ready to be in Mexico already.

I felt Cash tapping me on my shoulder to wake up no later than I had just closed my eyes. "Nigga, what?" I said, snapping my eyes open and giving him a death stare.

"Get yo' black ass up. We're here at the airport, and you too big for somebody to be carrying yo' ass." Cash jumped out of the driver's seat and headed to the trunk to unload our bags. We were finally at the damn airport. Seeing Fab and Jo' behind us holding hands while Fab carried their bags, I could see they must've connected more too on the way here. Jo' and Fab both had these big ass smiles on their faces, and I could tell they were happy together. I was so happy for them.

"Cancun, here we come, baby!" I screamed as we entered the airport.

"Shut yo' spoiled ass up. Don't be bringing all this attention to us. I have a surprise for you," Cash said, pulling me close to him.

"A surprise?" I was shocked because when did Cash ever do sweet shit like that?

"Yeah, but you need to wait until we get on the boat," Cash said, still holding on to me as we made our way through the airport.

FINALLY, we landed and were near the boat. Yes! We were going on a cruise! If I was going on any vacation, I needed to go all out because if I didn't, I just wouldn't feel right. I had never rode in a boat as big as this one before. It looked like a huge vacation

spot. It had its own pool, bar and grille, suites, and everything. Jo' and I were both in awe at how beautiful it was.

"I hate to admit this, but if I could, I would live here," Jo' said as we both entered our room.

"Whoa, wait, what are you doing, baby girl?" Fab said, looking at Jo' as she was about to place her bags down on the bed.

"What does it look like, Fab?" Jo' asked sarcastically.

"Nah, what I'm saying is you're sharing a room with me, not Bria, so grab yo' stuff and come on. Cash is staying with her. We'll link up with y'all later to go to the bar after we take a nap," Fab said, holding the door open for Jo'.

"That wasn't the fucking plan. Don't get here and start trying to switch stuff up!" I said, throwing a mini temper tantrum.

"Don't start, Bria. This trip isn't about all of that. Just enjoy your time with your man for a little bit, and we'll meet at the bar later," Fab emphasized. I guess I had no choice anyway. Cash was already unpacking his bags. This was going to be a wild trip and possibly the longest few days of my life.

"Granny? Is that you?" I was walking on the boat. I had just popped a Xanax and told Cash I wanted to get some fresh air, which was true. Being in the car with him the whole ride here, I needed time to clear my head.

Seeing my grandmother was odd because I hadn't seen her

since the funeral when we were putting her to rest. My grandmother was my backbone, and she had always been my go-to when it came to boys. For some reason, I never felt comfortable talking to my mom about it, and that was probably because she was barely around when we I was growing up with her odd jobs.

"Yes, baby, it's me. How are you? Why are you here?" Granny asked, walking closer to me. She pulled me in for a hug, and it took me back to the time when I was a little girl. I missed Granny so much, and I wished like hell I had spent more time with her. But now that I was getting the opportunity to do so, I wasn't going to just let her go so easily.

"I've been fine, Grandma. Just having guy issues. I miss you so much! You just don't understand. What do you mean why am I here? I'm on vacation with Fabio, Cash ,and my best friend, Josie."

"No, baby. You're in heaven with me. As much as I miss you, I can't let you stay here too long. You're needed back on earth. You're having guy troubles because you forgot the most important thing I told you that's efficient for a strong relationship," Granny added.

Did she just say I was in heaven? What the hell was that supposed to mean? I never heard that saying before. "Heaven, Granny? I'm confused. I remember everything you told me, and I'm trying so hard to put it into effect, but it's hard. Cash makes it so hard," I admitted.

"That's what I said. I don't know what happened to get you here, but you need to straighten up. Like I said, I miss you baby *girl but not that much where I need you up here with me so soon. I need grandbabies. You know I'm depending on you. That Fabio isn't going to settle down anytime, soon is he?"* I just ignored the part about being in heaven. I didn't want to go into detail about that when I could be talking to Granny about other stuff that I couldn't talk to anyone else about.

"Actually, Granny, I hooked him up with my friend, Josie. She's from Brazil, and they're actually hitting it off pretty well. Better than I expected, I think he's willing to change for her. Me, on the other hand, I've had the least of luck." *I revealed.*

"I'm proud of him. Tell him I'm keeping my fingers crossed on them two whenever you see them again. You know you've always been the type to put others before yourself. You out here trying to play matchmaker and can't even get yourself together. But that's what I loved about you the most; you have a heart of gold like your grandfather. Now, tell me what's been going on with you and that little boy, Cash," *Granny said, wasting no time to get to the bottom of things. That's what I loved about her. She was always ready to be there with a listening ear and a shoulder to cry on if you needed it.*

"Honestly, I love Cash, but I don't know, Granny. I feel like I'm going backward, and we aren't moving anywhere. He's tried apologizing to me so many times, and he tries so hard to try to make me happy, but it's always that thought in the back of my head that he's with someone else. I know you taught me to always follow my gut, and that's what I've been doing for the most part." *I felt the tears creeping up.*

"This is the time to let it all out, baby. You know granny will *never judge you. There is one thing that I see you're lacking, and I feel like if you really want to be with him, you'll make it work. You're the only one that has control over this situation. Do you think your grandfather was the best man? No, he was not. I had to build that man up into the man I wanted him to be. That isn't the case all the time, but sometimes, you need to learn to forgive. Y'all are both young. Things are going to happen, but as long as he has the utmost respect for you and he's trying, give him that credit," Granny said. Oh, how I missed these talks. I wished I could just stay here with her.*

"Granny, you know what? I really needed to hear that. I was so worried about what people would think of us. I mean, I don't have people in my business, but we are pretty known, and it seems like my life always finds its way to become public." I placed my head in my hands and just let the tears fall. I hadn't broken down like this in a long time, and it wasn't one of those sad cries. It was a happy cry because I finally got the answer I always wanted.

My granny was confirmation that I did deserve to be happy, and that I shouldn't care what people thought of me, because I was who I was. I just always felt like my life was always on the spotlight because of who my daddy was. The Wilsons weren't just your typical family. My dad helped the community, but he also hurt it in ways I didn't want to elaborate on. My grandmother knew because the game was like a family tradition in our lives.

Most families passed down college sweaters or football jerseys. My family passed down ownership of the streets. It was all a lot. I hated having to be hardcore all the time and hiding my emotions. So this cry felt good.

"Baby, you know I know I've been in this game longer than you. Way before you were thought about, believe me, I know how you feel. Come here, baby." Granny patted her lap with her hands as to summon me to lay my head in her lap. I used to always do that when I was younger. Granny died of a heart attack. The doctors said she had a bad heart since she was a little girl, but my grandmother was strong. She was a beautiful, strong black woman.

I looked up to her so much. Most of the women in the hood did shit. Granny was the head bitch in charge, as you would say. It didn't only hurt the family when she died. It hurt the hood. We all felt that, and I think it hurt me the most because she was the only person I could talk to about anything. She knew about Cash and me when she was alive, and she always told me she loved how he made me light up like a Christmas tree on Christmas morning just like Papa used to do her.

That always made me feel confident in what we had because if my grandmother knew, then it was real. She wouldn't just let me date anybody. "Granny, why can't I stay here with you?" I questioned. It was so peaceful here. I didn't have to worry about a thing here.

"Baby, your family needs you. They can't bury you too. Your dad is already going batshit crazy. You know that, right?" Granny did a long, hard chuckle.

"I miss that laugh, man. They don't need me. Dad is doing perfectly fine running the streets by his lonely. Fab is helping *him a lot with that now a days." I huffed. I wasn't jealous or anything. It was just that I wanted Fabio and I to have a different life. I wanted to be a normal person.*

"Chile, listen to me here, you haven't been through a thing yet. More bodies are going to fall. That's just how the game goes, but your biggest priority is doing what you can to make yourself happy. Don't let these chickenheads in her streets get in your head. How are you going to take on your granny's footsteps if you are letting people beneath you get to you? Lord, don't act like I haven't taught you anything." Granny began stroking my hair, causing my mind to stop racing.

"I'm listening, Granny. It's just a lot. But I got this. You know you taught me well, and I'm not going to let you down. I promise."

"I know you won't, because you know I'll always be watching you. On another note, I love Josie. Fabio needs to keep Nicki away from her and settle down for real. I'm going to tell you this, Josie isn't the one to be played with. She's sweet and innocent now, but he needs to not cross her. She's not going to sit around and wait on him to get it together. She's perfect for him. Tell him if he really wants to get it together, then he'll marry Josie, and you will keep her as your best friend. She's not these other females," Granny said.

I sat in thought for a moment and shrugged my shoulders. I didn't even go into details about her, but Granny knew. I wasn't going against anything she said, and I learned to never question her. We sat there for a few more moments talking about every- thing, and it was so reassuring to have her here.

12

Fabio "Fab"

With Bria being in a coma, it was like everything was on pause. I knew we should've left before the funeral, but Cambria was the one booking the flights, and she wanted to wait 'til after, and I was calling myself letting her get her way because of the whole shit she witnessed with Marquez. I knew I should've followed my gut, man.

Breaking the news to my mom and dad was the hardest because shit wasn't supposed to go down like this. It just wasn't. The past few weeks had been real low key. Gutta was nowhere to be found. It wasn't like I was looking for him though. I was ducked off with Josie.

Spending time with her had me not even concerned with all the bullshit. We just kicked it and watched movies. My mind couldn't help but worry about Cash. He was awake, but he wasn't able to walk. The doctors said the bullet traveled through his body, nipping a nerve on his spine. If he ever wanted to walk again, he was going to have to go through intense therapy.

I hadn't been up there in a few days, because he wasn't taking it too easy with Bria being in the coma. He was cursing out everybody that came his way, and he was constantly in her room, talking to her while holding her hand. The shit was so heart breaking. I felt like I had let my whole family down. This was truly a hard pill for the Wilson family.

"Babe, let's go see Bria. I miss her so much," Jo' said, rubbing my arm as if she was trying to comfort me. I'm sure she could tell something was up with me. I needed to find Hennessy and Nicki and handle their asses. I told them not to come near my family again, and they continued. I didn't give a fuck if Gutta fucked with them. When they put a bullet in my sister, I lost respect for all of them, and I wasn't taking anything lightly. Females or not.

"I'll drop you off up there, Jo'. I have something to handle, and I don't want to hold you up. I'll be up there later," I told Jo'.

"OK, well, that's fine. I guess." Jo' got up from the couch and headed to the bathroom. I could tell that she was feeling some type of way, but I really had to get this shit done. I said I wasn't going to do anything until Bria was awake, but sitting around on my ass was eating me up.

It took us an hour and a half to finish getting dressed. I was feeling really simple today. I threw on a white T-shirt and a pair of black slides. I watched Josie as she got dressed, and I couldn't help but to go up behind her and just pull her in my arms. These past few weeks haven't been easy for either of us, but here we were standing, fighting this shit together.

"Uh, no, don't be trying to be all lovey-dovey now, nigga," Jo' said, trying to get from my hold.

"Where you are going, baby girl?" I planted a kiss on her neck, and I could just tell by her body that she was no longer interested in trying to get away. "I said, where are you going? Can you answer me that?" I questioned, knowing she wasn't going to answer.

"Take me to the hospital before I get to swinging." Josie tried to hold her laugh in. It was still funny to me that she was talking the way she was starting to act more and more like Bria. I chuckled.

"Don't be laughing at me, Fabio." Josie cut her eyes at me.

"Come on, man, 'fore I tear yo' little ass up out of them clothes, and we don't make it anywhere." I quickly let her know.

"Boy, bye. I'm still going to see my best friend, regardless." Jo' brushed past me and headed to the car. I followed behind her.

Twenty minutes down the road, and we were finally arriving at the hospital. I felt the chills creep down my spine as I pulled into the parking spot. "Man." I huffed.

"I know, babe. This shit makes me feel crazy every time

I come up here. I still can't believe it. I'm just waiting for the day she wakes up," Jo' said.

"Me too, man. Me too," was all I could muster to say. I wasn't trying to break down in front of Jo', but this shit was killing me, man. So I just kept my words to a minimum.

"I love you, baby. Don't get into any trouble, and don't shed too many tears when I get out of this car. Have faith, papi. She's going to wake up. Promise." Jo' gave me this beautiful ass smile that I would never forget. That shit made a nigga feel good.

"I love you too, babe, and I won't. I'll be back soon. Tell Bria and Cash I said hey and I love them. I know you going to run into Cash. His ass always in her room," I added.

"Yeah, that's love though. If anything ever happens to me, you better be the same way too. I'm not playing," Jo' said as she closed the passenger door and headed into the hospital.

Jo' was the only thing that kept me going in this hard time, but it was time for me to shake this shit and try to find Nicki and Hennessy. I knew they weren't in hiding because Pops told me someone told him that she was last seen at the corner store near her house.

The bullet that hit her only had her in a damn sling while my sister and brother were suffering. When I pulled up to Nicki's house, I wasn't surprised to see her raggedy ass Honda out front. I tried to coach myself to remain calm because there was a 100% chance that my daughter was in there.

I took no time peeping my surroundings before I made any moves. I was alone, so I had to make sure I was on my P's and Q's for sure. I was just going to rough her up a little bit. Walking up the driveway I could see that Nicki had already seen me walking up because she was standing at the door with her arms crossed.

"Why are you on my property, and you shot my cousin, dummy? Back the fuck up." Nicki waved her gun at me. The closer I walked, the more I realized it was a water gun.

"Girl, you ain't gon' shoot shit. You knew we were going to run into each other sometime." I swiftly walked up to her door and let myself in.

"Just because you're my baby daddy doesn't mean you can come to my house whenever you want." Nicki rolled her eyes.

"Where is my daughter?" I questioned, ignoring what she had just said.

"At my mother's, why?" Nicki cut her eyes at me, and that's when I took the initiative to turn and face her. She looked like she had been crying, and this just wasn't any regular cry.

"What's wrong with you?" I asked. For some reason, I was concerned at why she looked so down. I wasn't used to seeing her like this, so it threw me off guard.

"I don't want to talk about it. What do you want, Fab?" Nicki tried to bat away the tears in her eyes.

"Just because I don't fuck with you don't mean you can't vent to me as long as that shit ain't out of line or about Jo' or Cambria. I mean, you are still my child's mother."

I don't know what came over me, but in reality, Nicki and I didn't fall off on bad terms. I just couldn't fuck with her because I couldn't trust her. I watched as she looked at me and then looked away.

"See, there you go, worried about that girl. Do you even care that we let this shit get too far? Do you even care that I still love you? Like I mean, I've never done anything out the way to harm you, Fab! I just don't understand why I'm getting the short end of the stick. This girl just stepped foot in Atlanta, and you ready to risk it all for her. Like what's good with you? Never seen you so stuck up somebody's ass like this." Nicki sat on the arm of her chair and put her head in her hands.

She was right though. A lot of shit did come between us that shouldn't have, but she wasn't about to sit here and blame all of that on Jo'. My vibe with Jo' could never be explained, and I wasn't about to sit and go back and forth with my ex trying to explain my love for my new shorty. That just wasn't something I was about to do.

"Nicki, look, you act like this little 'relationship, co-parenting' thing we have going on has always been easy. It hasn't. We fell off because it just wasn't in me to keep forcing shit with you. Don't get me wrong, I got love for you, but it's nothing like what I feel for Jo', and I'm not about to sit here and try to explain that to you. Actually, I didn't come here for none of this actually," I admitted.

"I know, Fab. I know. I just don't get why I'll never be good enough to be in your world. I'm still madly in love with you, and I'm not asking you to explain anything. You don't have to. This shit just hit different when your baby daddy is really trying to move on." Nicki started crying, and this time I could really see the hurt all over her face. Nicki had never been so vulnerable before. I walked up to her and grabbed her hand to comfort her.

"Look, ma, all that crying shit is irrelevant. So stop it," I said. Nicki pulled me by my belt buckle, so my dick was right in her face.

"Can we fuck one last time?" Nicki said, almost making me smack the fuck out of her goofy ass. Nicki knew what time it was now. She never understood that when someone was being there for her that, that's all it was. She always wanted to go the extra mile, and I wasn't fucking with it.

"What are you doing? All this crying shit was just a front?" I smacked her hand away from my belt.

"Come on, Fab. You act like you don't miss this pussy." Nicki purred as she walked closer to me.

"Nah, I'm not acting. I'm good on you." I pulled my gun out and sat it right in the middle of her forehead, and I watched as all the color escaped her face.

"Please, Fab, I'm sorry." Nicki's tune changed real quick.

"Nah, you aren't though, because you keep doing the same shit and keep overstepping. I've told you too many times to stop disrespecting me, but you don't listen." I changed positions of the cut and knocked her across her face with the butt of the gun. She fell to the floor, holding her face and crying, but this time, I didn't even give a fuck. I was back to reality, and I remembered exactly what I came to do.

"That bitch got you acting like this? Alright, bet." Nicki wiped the blood from her upper lip. "Get the fuck out!" Nicki screamed.

"She doesn't have me acting like shit. My sister is in a fucking coma. That's what got me acting the way I do. I told you not to come near her, and I'm letting you slide because you wasn't the one to pull the trigger, but if you step foot near her again, I'll be forced to bury you right next to yo' dead ass daddy and be forced to take custody of Aubrey. I mean, shit, she probably wouldn't mind having Jo' as a stepmom. You don't spend time with her no way." I spat as I exited.

I could tell what I said had struck a nerve with Nicki, but I didn't give a fuck. She lost her daddy to this street shit, so she knew what would be in store for her ass. This was my last and final warning.

13

Josie "Jo"

I hated seeing my best friend like this. Bria didn't deserve any of this at all. I just felt like we were all at the wrong place at the wrong time. I sat at her bedside, holding her hand. I was trying to hold back my tears because this wasn't what she needed right now, but I couldn't help it.

"Bria, if you can hear me, enough is enough now. I need you to wake up. I miss you. I really need to talk to you about something." I was referring to the shit that happened with Gutta at the cookout after the funeral. I hadn't told Fab yet, and it wasn't doing anything but eating away at me.

I knew it wasn't a good time, and that's all that I kept thinking about. I always had an issue with putting other people's problems before mine. I hadn't had sex with Fab since it happened, and he didn't question me about it once. That's how I knew then that both of our minds were on other shit. The past few weeks, all we did was lay up and watch movies. I really enjoyed the quality time we spent together because I know without him, I didn't know how I was going to keep it together.

I was a little upset he didn't want to come to the hospital, but I guess I could understand where he was coming from. I heard Bria's door open, and that's when I saw Cash rolling in, in his wheelchair. "Hey, Cash. How are you?" I asked.

"I could be better. I was in physical therapy today. But I couldn't even focus enough to keep my mind off Bria," Cash replied.

I knew what that meant; it was another unsuccessful day. I felt for him so much because it was a lot to take in. I just shook my head at his response because I didn't want him to take anything I said the wrong way.

"Anyway, any update with Bria?" Cash rolled to the side of her bed and grabbed her hand, and I watched as he kissed it.

"Not yet. This shit is so depressing and stressful. I just want her to wake up so bad." I felt the knots in my throat as I switched my attention back to her. I could no longer fight the tears as I let them flow. Everything was just piling up on me between my family, Gutta, and now Cambria. I just needed to let it out.

"Jo', chill, man. You know Fab would lose it if he saw you crying like this. Where is he at anyway? Do you have something you need to get off of your chest?"

"He's out handling something, but I think he's just avoiding seeing y'all like this. He's really been beating himself up about the whole situation. On another note, I do need to talk to someone about something that happened to me," I admitted with the tears still full in my eyes.

"I need him to come see me, man. I need to talk to my brother. None of this was his fault. I've been beating myself up every night since this shit happened. I just hope Cambria can find a way to forgive me. I love her with everything in me, and when she wakes up from this, I just want to make it completely official with her. I want to buy a crib so we can move in it together. Besides that, what's up with you? What happened, Jo'?" Cash asked with concern in his voice.

It was so sweet how he talked about Bria and how everything was starting to make sense to him now. I knew that when Bria woke up, she was going to forgive him because he basically took a bullet for her too. Yeah, she got hit too, but this was going to make their relationship stronger no doubt.

"When he comes to get me, I'll make sure he comes in. That's so sweet how you talk about Bria. Don't stress when she comes up out of this. She's going to be happy to see you by her bedside. I know if a nigga takes a bullet for me, he's going to be my husband because that's a nigga that'll do anything for you, simple as that. Well, I haven't told Fab yet, because too much has been going on, but after the funeral, when we left to go get drinks…" I stopped because the thought of the way Gutta held me down and took advantage of me was making me sick on my stomach.

"Jo', talk, man. Don't start some shit and not finish, and why haven't you told Fab? Is it that serious? Man, I swear to God if somebody put they hands on you, me and Fab going to make sure they meet they motherfucking maker. Now tell me." I could see the anger displaying on Cash's face. I almost didn't want to say it, but I know I needed to.

"Gutta raped me," I blurted out just as Fab was walking in the door. I didn't know he was coming so soon he didn't tell me he was on the way.

"What the fuck did you just say?" Fab walked closer to me, not turning his attention away.

"Please don't make me repeat it," I cried.

"How? When? Why didn't you tell me, Jo'? This isn't some shit you just brush under the rug. I'm going to kill that nigga, man. Pops don't even have to worry about it. I was going to chill, but I'm not letting up. Niggas want to act crazy? I'm going to show them crazy!" Fab huffed.

"I didn't want you to find out like this. I wanted to tell you, Fab, but I know you already have a lot on your plate right now. I didn't want to be a burden," I explained.

"Babe, don't ever think you're a burden to me. You

remember me telling you that'll I'd do anything to protect you? I meant that shit for real. Anything." Fab pulled me up from my seat and pulled me in for a tight hug. Standing there in his arms, everything felt so reassuring, and I didn't reflect so much on the pain anymore because I wasn't trying to hold it in.

"I love you, Fab," I said before I even noticed it slipped out. Oh my God, what did I just do? I quickly pulled away from him and dropped my face to the ground, trying to avoid him.

"Awww, shit!" Cash said. I almost forgot that he was in the room. Fab had that effect on me sometimes, made me feel like the only girl in the world.

"Shut up, nigga. I love you too, Jo'," Fab replied. I stood there for a moment, not replying. I wasn't ready to. I felt like he was just saying it because I had said it, even though he showed me in many ways this past year since I had been in Atlanta that he had love for me. But I just wasn't so sure right now. There we were, all gathered around Bria's bed, and I knew we were all hoping for the best that she would wake up.

We finally left the hospital around four. I really didn't want to leave, but I did need a nap, and I must admit I was tired of crying, and I just wanted to take a hot bubble bath. Every day felt like a long day without my best friend. I missed her loud, goofy self. Bria always brightened my moods, and she would always tell me the right thing to do.

I prayed to God on the way home because I just wanted Him to make a way. I think I had been through enough.

"Baby girl, tonight, I want to make you feel good. These past few weeks I've been in my feelings and not noticing that you're falling apart. I'm so sorry." Fab broke the silence.

"It's alright, Fab. I know you got your shit too. I'll never fault you for this."

"Get undressed," Fab added as we stepped into the master bedroom of his apartment.

"Wait? Huh?" I questioned. He was so random.

"Take them off. Now. Let me see how beautiful you are." Fab walked up to me and started to pull my clothes off piece by piece. I hadn't felt like having sex since Gutta, but Fab was turning me on something I couldn't resist. Then he pulled away from me and walked in the bathroom turning on the bath water.

"What are you doing? I thought—"

"You thought you was about to get some dick, didn't you?" Fab chuckled at my facial expression. I know I had the craziest look on my face because I really thought he was about to drop dick all in me, but I guess I thought wrong.

He ran the bath water, added some bubbles, and then watched me step in. He told me to relax. This shit felt so good as I let the bubbles relax my body. It was crazy how Fab knew exactly what I needed, and I was just thinking about it.

"Here, beautiful." Fab handed me a wine glass full of Jose Cuervo.

"Fab?" I looked at it and laughed and blushed at the same time.

"Hush, don't ruin a real-nigga moment. I'm doing something new, and this is all I had downstairs." Fab smirked. I took this time to admire how sculpted his face was. He was really a handsome man with toffee-brown skin, long, shoulder-length dreads, and hazel-green eyes. I couldn't help but stare at his full, pink lips and pearly-white teeth every time he smiled.

"You're so romantic. I didn't know you had this side to you," I admitted.

"A nigga got a little something in him."

"You know when I said I loved you earlier? I really meant that. I know we're still new and stuff, but I just want you to know that it's the truth. I don't want you to feel pressured to say anything to me that you don't mean. I just needed to get that off my chest." I revealed.

"Hold up. Wait. Where is this coming from?" Fab brought his eyebrows together as if he was confused. I mean, it was a random statement, but I wanted him to know how I really felt. I was done being the shy, unspoken Jo'. It was time for a change, and I wanted everybody to feel me regardless.

"This is how I feel. I just don't want you saying something you aren't sure that you mean. I know it could be a lot of pressure from just those three words," I said.

"Well, let me tell you how I feel, since this is what we are doing. I fuck with you hard, and I can't deny that. I don't tell people I love them if I don't mean it. I know we've only known each other for a bit, but what I feel is real. No cap in my rap. If I'm fucking with you, that's that. End of discussion. Don't question my love again, girl, I'll do anything for you. Most of the shit I've done, I haven't done for anybody else. I mean what I say." Fab held my hand in his and planted a kiss on my forehead. I sat there for another thirty minutes just talking to him about our future and relaxing.

"I won't question you on that again, because your actions speak louder, but I will tell you as soon as you start moving funny, I'm going to question yo' ass as many times as I want," I added.

"Don't worry about that, lil' mama. My actions would never have you questioning where we stand," Fab mentioned. He made me feel so secure.

The way this man made me feel, I knew for a fact it was meant to be. He's was so perfect to me, and I wouldn't trade him for anyone else. I was so happy that we had this time to get to know each other. I climbed out of the tub, and Fab lead my naked body to the bed. I laid on my stomach while he oiled me down with baby oil.

"Mmm, this feels so good," I moaned as he massaged every inch of my body.

"It's way more of this later down the line. This is just the beginning, baby girl, I'm telling you. I'm going to pamper you in so many ways. Show you how a woman is supposed to be treated," Fab added.

I loved the good shit he was talking. I just let it all sink in. We ended up drifting off to sleep, and I couldn't have been anymore happier than I was right now. All I needed was my best friend.

14

Fabio "Fab"

Another month had passed, and my baby sister was still in a coma. The doctor said she was starting to come around a little, but she still wasn't out of the woods. I was feeling confident though because she was starting to make small movements, like twitching movements. I was still not going to the hospital as much, because it was depressing.

I went to see Cash a few times, and we chopped it up, but he was still struggling with his physical therapy. It was crazy because any minute, you could be in a wheelchair. I couldn't even imagine how he felt. I just wished my nigga the best.

Today was the day I was going to spend time with my momma. She wanted to talk to me about something, but I just figured it was something about Bria. My mom and pops were putting a lot of money into her medical bills. It wasn't easy. I assumed she just needed some extra help.

"Hey, Mom! What's up? How you and Pops holding up?" I asked, even though I was already well aware of her standing with the whole situation.

My mom's hair was all over her head, her eyes were red and puffy, and I could just see she wasn't herself. My mom never went anywhere without her head done. I swear as long as I could remember, my mom always kept her hair up.

"I'm trying, baby. It's hard. I called you over here because I have something important to talk to you about. This is completely your choice, but your father has the official final say so," my mom said, losing me completely.

"Huh? My father? Pops? Ma, what are you talking about?" I sat down next to her on the couch where she was previously patting for me to sit.

"No, toot. Your biological father, Alfonzo Alberto in Brazil, papi. He's getting sicker, and he needs you to come lead the cartel for a bit until he gets better, if he gets better. If there is one thing I know about your dad, it's that he loves to downplay situations. Just like when your mother was real down and sick, he downplayed that shit until he couldn't anymore. You'll have to contact him and let him know your plan by the end of this week," my mom said.

I was still in shock. Did she just say I had to lead a fucking cartel? I didn't know shit about that. I was a street nigga. My pops hadn't reached out to me this whole time, but now he wanted me to handle his business?

"Nah. Shit ain't going down like that. He can't make me do shit. That nigga don't even communicate with me. The fuck!" I replied.

"Watch your tone, Fabio! He's still your father, and I'm still your biological mother. I think you should do it," my mom added. I looked at her like she had three heads. She was really talking out the side of her neck.

"Ma, I don't got time for this. Just send me his number. I'll holla at him." I got up and left. I felt bad for leaving her there like that, but she was dropping bomb after bomb. I couldn't take all of this. I was just trying to process all of this shit.

Jo' and I had just started to know each other better. Things were alright for us right now, besides Cash and Bria. I didn't need this bullshit in my life at this moment.

15

Josie "Jo'"

Fabio told me he was going to see his mother before he came to pick me up, which was fine. I had spent the night with Bria, and I wouldn't mind some more time. With the doctor saying that she could wake up any day now, I wanted to be the first one to be there when she did.

My phone started ringing, and I saw it was Fab. Apparently, he had butt dialed me because when I continuously said hello, he didn't say anything.

"Hello? Fab? Babe, are you there?" It sounded like he was in an argument with someone, so I sat to listen to see if he was alright. When I heard his mom say he had to call his biological father about taking the throne as the leader of the cartel in Brazil that killed my whole family, I dropped my phone to the floor, causing the screen to crack. I felt like my whole heart had stopped...

To Be Continued...

AUTHOR'S NOTE

Thanks to everyone who downloaded and read my book. I really appreciate you guys so much. This book for me means a lot because not only did I take my time writing this, but I felt like I overcame so much writing this book. Majority of the characters I can relate to on a personal level simply because I've been through a few of the same situations. Leave a review, and let me know what you guys think. This book is only part one with more to come. Number 7 down with many more to come. Join my reading group on Facebook at "Books N Tingz by Precious T". Again, thanks to everyone who supported this release. It means so much.

CPSIA information can be obtained
at www.ICGtesting.com
Printed in the USA
LVHW091509170519
618250LV00003B/401/P

9 781095 532003